She reminded him of a sea nymph.

It wasn't until this moment that Jake noticed just how beautiful Lily was. Her long hair was a rich shade of mahogany, and he'd rarely seen it unbound. But today, Lily had left it free so that it fell in gentle waves around her shoulders.

But what Jake loved most about Lily were her eyes. Never in his life had he met anyone with eyes so dark and expressive. Some days they were like cellophane, and he could read her moods as clearly as the words in a book.

He could imagine what it would be like making love to her. He wouldn't need to see anything but her eyes to... What was the matter with him? He was looking at Lily like a prospective lover.

Dear Reader,

Welcome to Silhouette. Experience the magic of the wonderful world where two people fall in love. Meet heroines who will make you cheer for their happiness, and heroes (be they the boy next door or a handsome, mysterious stranger) who will win your heart. Silhouette Romances reflect the magic of love—sweeping you away with books that will make you laugh and cry, heartwarming, poignant stories that will move you time and time again.

In the next few months, we're publishing romances by many of your all-time favorites, such as Diana Palmer, Brittany Young, Emilie Richards and Arlene James. Your response to these authors and other authors of Silhouette Romances has served as a touchstone for us, and we're pleased to bring you more books with Silhouette's distinctive medley of charm, wit and—above all—*romance*.

I hope you enjoy this book and the many stories to come. Experience the magic!

Sincerely,

Tara Hughes
Senior Editor
Silhouette Books

DEBBIE MACOMBER
Friends—
And Then Some

Silhouette *Romance*

Published by Silhouette Books New York

America's Publisher of Contemporary Romance

SILHOUETTE BOOKS
300 E. 42nd St., New York, N.Y. 10017

Copyright © 1986 by Debbie Macomber

ISBN: 0-373-08474-9

First Silhouette Books printing December 1986

America's Publisher of Contemporary Romance

Printed in the U.S.A.

DEBBIE MACOMBER

has quickly become one of Silhouette's most prolific authors. As a wife and mother of four, she not only manages to keep her family happy, but she also keeps her publisher and readers happy with each book she writes.

SAN FRANCISCO AND ENVIRONS

Berkeley

Samuel P. Taylor
State Park

Bay Bridge

Oakland

Golden Gate Bridge

Fisherman's
Wharf

Golden Gate Park

San Francisco Bay

PACIFIC
OCEAN

OREGON

IDAHO

Sacramento

NEVADA

San Francisco

Fresno

CALIFORNIA

ARIZONA

Los Angeles

San Diego

Chapter One

The thick canvas sail flapped in the breeze before Jake Carson aligned the boat to catch the wind. The *Lucky Lady* responded by slicing through the choppy waters of San Francisco Bay. Satisfied, Jake leaned back and closed his eyes, content with his life and with the world.

"Do you think I'm being terribly mercenary?" Lily Morrissey asked as she stretched her legs out and crossed them at the ankles. "It sounds so coldhearted to decide to marry a man simply because he's wealthy. But I've decided he doesn't have to be *that* rich. Only the other day I was thinking about that." She paused to sigh expressively. Lately she'd given the matter some consideration. For almost a year now she'd been playing the piano at the Wheaton. Only wealthy men could afford to stay at a hotel as expensive as the Wheaton. And Lily was determined to find herself such a man. Unfortunately, no one had leaped forward, and she'd grown discouraged. Each day she told herself that she would meet someone soon. That hope was what kept Lily going back night after night.

"I'd only want someone rich enough to appreciate opera," she added thoughtfully. "Naturally it'd be nice if he drove a Mercedes, but that isn't essential. All I really care about is his bank account. It's got to be large enough to take care of Gram and me. That doesn't sound so bad, does it?"

A faint smile tugged at the corners of Jake's mouth.

"Jake?" she repeated, slightly irritated.

"Hmm?"

"You haven't heard a word I said."

"Sure I have. You were talking about finding yourself a wealthy man."

"Yes, but that's what I always talk about. You could have guessed." Maybe she was foolish to dream of the day when a generous man would adorn her with diamonds and wrap her in furs—nothing like that old muskrat thing her grandmother wore. Lily knew that she was meant for mink and fox and three-karat diamond rings.

"I wasn't guessing. I heard every word."

Lily studied him through narrowed eyes. "Sure you did," she mumbled under her breath.

Jake's slow, lazy smile came into play again.

Lily studied the profile of her best friend. Jake drove a taxi and they'd met the first week she worked at the Wheaton. She owed him a lot. Not only did he give her free rides back and forth to work when he was available, which was just about every day, but he'd rescued Gram and Lily from the Wheaton's manager.

Lily's starting salary had been less than what Gram had paid for an hour of piano lessons. Gram had raised Lily from the time her mother had died and her father had sought his fortune as a merchant marine. Gram had been outraged by the manager's unintended slight. And Gram, being Gram, couldn't do anything without a production. She'd shown up at the hotel in authentic witch doctor's costume and proceeded to chant a voodoo rite of retribution over the manager's head.

Luckily, Lily had gotten her grandmother out of the lobby before the police arrived. Jake had been standing next to his taxi and had witnessed the entire scene. Before everything exploded in Lily's face, Jake held open the cab door and whisked Gram and Lily away from any unpleasantness. Over the months that followed, the three had become good friends.

Jake was actually a struggling writer. He lived on board his boat and worked hard enough to meet expenses by driving the taxi. He didn't seem to take anything too seriously. Not even his writing. Lily sometimes wondered how many other people he gave free rides to. Money didn't matter to Jake. But it did to Lily.

"I *am* going to meet someone," Lily continued on a serious note.

"I don't doubt it," Jake said and yawned, raising his hand to cover his mouth.

"I mean it, Jake. Tonight. I bet I meet someone tonight."

"For your sake, I hope you're right," Jake mumbled in reply.

Her words echoed in her ears several hours later when Lily pulled out the bench of the huge grand piano that dominated the central courtyard of the

Wheaton. Dressed in her full-length sequined gown and dainty slippers, she was barely recognizable as the woman who'd spent the afternoon aboard Jake's boat.

Deftly her fingers moved over the smooth ivory keys as her upper body swayed with the melody of an old Karen Carpenter hit.

Some days Lily felt that her smile was as artificial as her thick, curling eyelashes. After twenty-seven hundred times of hearing "Moon River," "Misty" and "Sentimental Journey," Lily was ready to take a journey herself. Maybe that was why she had talked to Jake. If she was going to meet someone, surely she would have by now. Sighing inwardly, she continued playing, hardly conscious of her fingers.

Five minutes later when Lily glanced up, she was surprised to find a ruddy faced cowboy standing next to the piano, watching her.

She smiled up at him and asked. "Is there something you'd like to hear?" He had to be close to forty, with the beginnings of a double chin. A huge turquoise buckle dominated the slight thickening at his waist. He was a good-looking man who was already going to seed.

"Do you know 'Santa Fe Gal of Mine'?" The slight Southern drawl wasn't a surprise. His head was topped with a Stetson although he was dressed in an oversize-plaid linen sport coat that hadn't cost a penny under five hundred dollars. A Texan, she mused; a rich Texan, probably into oil.

"'Santa Fe Gal of Mine,'" she repeated aloud. "I'm not sure that I do know it," she answered with a warm smile. "Hum a few bars for me." She didn't usually get many requests. People were more interested in checking into the hotel or meeting their friends for a drink in the sunken cocktail lounge to care about what she was playing.

The man placed a steadying hand against the side of the piano and momentarily closed his eyes. "I can't remember the melody," he admitted sheepishly. "Sorry, I'm not much good with that sort of thing."

Lily got a glance at his feet and recognized the shoes from an advertisement she'd seen in *Gentlemen's Quarterly*. Cowboy boots, naturally, but ones made of imported leather and inlaid with silver. Leather, Lily felt, made the difference between being dressed and well dressed. This gentleman was definitely well dressed.

"Do you know who sang the popular version?" she questioned brightly, her heart pounding so hard it felt as though it would slam right out of her chest. She'd told Jake she was going to meet someone. And that someone was here at last!

"Nope, I can't say that I do."

"Maybe there's another song you'd like to hear?" Without conscious thought her hands continued to play yesteryear's hit as she looked up at the cowboy with two chins and reminded herself that looks weren't everything. But, then again, maybe he was married and had a son her age—an heir.

"One day I'm going to find some sweet gal who knows that blasted song," he muttered. "It always was my favorite."

Already Lily's mind had shifted into overdrive. Somehow, someway, she'd locate his long-lost song and gain his everlasting gratitude. "Will you be around tomorrow?"

"I should be."

"Come back and I'll see what I can do."

He straightened and gave her a brief salute. "I'll do that, little filly."

Lily's heart was pounding so hard that by the time she finished an hour later, she felt as if she'd been doing calisthenics. Maybe he'd be so grateful he'd insist on taking her to dinner. This could be the break Lily had waited months for. It hadn't happened exactly as she'd expected, but it was just the chance she'd been wanting. Already she could picture herself sitting in an elegant restaurant, ordering almond-saffron soup and lobster in wine sauce. For dessert she'd have Italian ice cream with walnuts and caramel sauce oozing from the sides. Her mouth watered just thinking about all the wonderful foods she'd read about but never tasted. Her Texan would probably order barbecued chicken, but she wouldn't care. He could well be her ticket to riches and a genteel life...if she played her cards right. And for the first time in a long while, Lily felt she'd been dealt a hand of aces.

Jake was in his cab, parked in front of the hotel when she stepped into the balmy summer night. Eagerly she waved and hurried across the wide circular driveway to the bright-yellow taxi.

"Jake!" she cried. "Didn't I tell you today was the day? Didn't I? The most fantastically wonderful thing has happened! I can't believe I'm so lucky." She felt like holding out her arms and twirling around and bursting into song.

With one elbow leaning against the open window, Jake studied her with serious dark eyes and a slow, measured smile that lifted one corner of his full mouth. "Obviously Daddy Warbucks introduced himself."

"Yes," she giggled. "*My* Daddy Warbucks."

Leaning across the front seat, Jake swung open the passenger door. "Climb in and you can tell me all about it on the way to your house."

Rushing around the front of the car, Lily scooted inside the cab and closed the door. Jake started the engine and pulled onto the busy street, skillfully merging with the flowing traffic. "I was so surprised, I nearly missed my chance," Lily started up again. "Suddenly, after all these months, he was there in a five-hundred-dollar sport coat, requesting a song. He called me 'little filly,' and Jake, he's rich. Really, really rich. I can just see that Texas oil oozing from every pore." She paused long enough to inhale before continuing. "He's older, maybe forty, but that's not so bad. And he's nice. I can tell that about a man. Remember how I met you and instantly knew what a great person you were? That's just the kind of feeling I had tonight." She continued chattering for another full minute until she realized how quiet Jake had become. "Oh, Jake, I'm sorry, I've been talking up a storm here and barely giving you a chance to think."

"You're talking with a drawl."

"Oh, yeah, I'm practicing. I was born in Texas, you know."

"You were?"

"No, of course not, but I thought it'd impress him."

The slow, lazy smile came into play again.

Lily studied the intense profile of her friend as he steered. Jake wasn't handsome—not in the way the models for *Gentlemen's Quarterly* were. He was tall with broad shoulders and a muscular build. But with those sea-green eyes and that dark hair, he probably could be devastating if he tried. Only Jake couldn't care less. Half the time he dressed in faded jeans and outdated sweaters. Lily doubted that he even owned a suit. Formal wear wasn't in keeping with Jake's image.

As she studied Jake, Lily realized that she really didn't know much about him. Jake kept the past to himself. She knew he'd served in Vietnam as a medic, and had an engineering degree from a prestigious college back east someplace. From tidbits of conversation here and there, she'd learned that he'd worked at every type of job imaginable. There didn't seem to be anything he hadn't tried once and—if he liked it—done it again and again. In some ways Jake reminded Lily of her father who had been in the merchant marine and brought her a storehouse of treasures from around the world. Jake was the kind of man who could do anything he put his mind to. He was creative and intelligent, proud and resourceful. Lily supposed she loved him. He was her tried and true friend, her confidant and in many ways, her partner. Of course her feelings were more like those of a young girl for an endearing older brother or an adventurous sidekick. Love was an emotion Lily was holding in reserve for her husband. But first she had to convince a rich man that she would be an excellent wife.

Studying Jake now, Lily noted that something had displeased him. She could tell by the way he tucked back his chin, giving an imitation of a cobra prepared to strike. He was in a state of coiled alertness that exuded impatience and restrained anger. Yet there remained an aura of disciplined control in every action. From past experience, Lily knew that whatever was bothering him would be divulged in his own time and in his own way.

"Well?" he snapped.

"Well, what?"

"Are you going to tell me about J. Paul Getty or not?"

"Are you sure you want to hear? You sound like you want to snap my head off."

"Damn it, Lily, one of these days..." He paused to inhale sharply as if the night were responsible for his wrath. Several moments passed before he spoke, and when he did his voice was as smooth as velvet, almost caressing.

Lily wasn't fooled. Jake was furious. "All right, tell me what's wrong. Did you get stiffed again? I thought you had a foolproof system for avoiding that."

"No one stiffed me."

"Then what?"

He ignored her, seeming to concentrate on the traffic. "Listen, kid, you've got to be careful."

Lily hated it when Jake called her "kid" and he knew it. "Be careful? What are you talking about? You're acting like I'm planning to handle toxic waste. Good grief, I don't even know his name."

"You could be playing with fire."

"I'm not playing anything yet. Which reminds me, have you ever heard the song 'Santa Fe Gal of Mine'?"

"'Santa Fe Gal of Mine'?" The harsh disgruntled look left his expression as a smile split his mouth. "No, I can't say that I have."

"Gram will know it," Lily said with complete confidence. Her grandmother might be a bit eccentric, but the woman was a virtual warehouse of useless information. If that wealthy Texan's favourite song was ever on the charts, Gram would be able to tell her anything she needed to know.

Jake eased to a stop in front of the large two-story house with the wide front porch.

"Can you come in now or will you be by later?"

"Later," he answered with apparent indifference.

Lily walked toward the house and paused on the front steps, confused again. A disturbing shiver trembled through her at the cool, appraising way Jake had behaved this evening. His smooth, impenetrable green eyes resembled the dark jade Buddha her father had brought her from Hong Kong. Nothing about Jake had been the same tonight. Lily attributed it to his having had a bad day. But it shouldn't have been. They'd spent the majority of it sailing and they both loved that. But then everyone had a bad day now and again. Jake was entitled to his.

Shaking off the feelings of unease, Lily stepped inside the fifty-year-old house, pausing to pat Herbie. Herbie was her grandmother's favorite conversation piece—a shrunken head from South America. A zebra-skin rug from Africa rested in front of the fireplace.

The television blared from Gram's bedroom, but the older woman was snoring just as loudly, drowning out the sounds of the cops-and-robbers movie. With an affectionate smile, Lily turned off the set and quietly tiptoed from the darkened room. She'd talk to Gram in the morning.

After changing out of the red sequined gown, Lily inspected her limited wardrobe, wondering what she'd wear first if the Texan asked her to dinner. Possibly the gold lamé number with the plunging neckline. No, she mentally argued with herself. That dress could give him the wrong impression. The lavender chiffon one she'd picked up at Repeaters, a secondhand store, looked good with her dark eyes and had a high neckline. On reconsidering, Lily felt it would be best to start this relationship off right. Lily was a good girl.

She was sitting beside the old upright piano, sorting through Gram's sheet music that was stored in the bench when Jake returned. He let himself in, hung his jacket on the elephant tusks and picked up a discarded Glenn Miller piece from the top of the pile.

"Hi."

"Hi." At least he sounded in a better mood than earlier. "It'd be just like Gram to have that song and not even know it."

"You're determined to find it, aren't you?" Jake asked with a faint smile.

"I've got to find it," Lily shot back. "Everything will be ruined if I don't." Her sharp words bounced back without penetrating his aloof composure. "Don't you see? He won't be grateful if I can't find that song."

Jake sat on the arm of the sofa and idly flipped through the stack she'd already sorted. He didn't like the sounds of this Texan. He wasn't sure what he was feeling. Lily was determined to find herself a rich man and, knowing her persistence, Jake thought she probably would. When Lily wanted something, she went after it with unwavering resolve. In his life, there wasn't anything he cared that much about. Sure, there were things he wanted, but nothing that was worth abandoning the easygoing existence he had now. Lily's dark-brown eyes had sparkled with eager excitement when she'd told him about the Texan. He'd never seen anyone's eyes light up the way Lily's did.

"Did you get a chance to do any writing today?"

Jake straightened the tall stack of sheet music and sat upright. "I finished that short story I was telling you about and mailed it off."

Lily smiled up at him, her attention diverted for the moment. Jake had talent, but he wasted it on short stories that didn't sell when he should be concentrating on a novel. That's where the real money was. "Are you going to let me read this one?" He usually gave her his work to look over, mainly for grammar and spelling errors—Jake was a "creative" speller.

"Later," he hedged, not knowing why. He preferred it when Lily had a chance to correct his blatant errors, but there was something of himself in this story that he'd held in reserve, not wishing her to see. The interesting part of being a writer was that Jake didn't always like the people inside him who appeared on paper. Some were light and witty while others were dark and dangerous. None were like him and yet each one was a part of himself.

"I know Gram's got tons more sheet music than this," Lily mumbled, thoughtfully chewing on her bottom lip. "Do you want to go to the attic with me?"

"Sure."

He followed her up the creaky stairs to the second floor, then moved in front and opened the door that led to another staircase, this one narrower and steeper. Lily tucked her index finger in Jake's belt loop as the light from the hallway dimmed. They were surrounded by the pitch-black dark, two steps into the attic.

"Where's the light?"

An eerie sensation slowly crept up Lily's arm and settled in her stomach. The air was still with a stagnant heaviness. "In the center someplace. Jake, I'll do this tomorrow. It's creepy up here."

"We're here now," he argued and half turned, bringing her to his side and loosely taking her by the hand. "Don't worry, I'll protect you."

"Yeah, that's what I'm afraid of." She tried to make light of her apprehensions, and managed to squelch the urge to turn back toward the dim hallway light. Involuntarily she shivered. "Gram's got some weird stuff up here."

"It can't be any worse than what's downstairs," he murmured, and chuckled softly as he edged their way into the black void, taking short steps as he swung his hand out in front of him to prevent a collision with some inanimate object.

Gradually, Lily's eyes adjusted to the lack of light. "I think I see the string—to your left there." She pointed for his benefit and squeezed her eyes half-closed for a better view. It didn't look exactly right, but it could be the light.

"That's a hangman's noose."

"Good grief, what's Gram doing with that?" In some ways, she'd rather not know what treasures Gram had stored up here. The attic was Gram's territory and Lily hadn't paid it a visit in years. In truth, Lily didn't really want to know what her sweet grandmother was doing with a hangman's noose.

"She told me once that her grandfather is said to have ridden with Jesse James. The noose might have something to do with that." As he spoke, Jake's foot collided with a box and he stumbled forward a few steps until he regained his balance.

Lily let out a sharp gasp, then held her breath. "Are you all right?"

"I'm fine."

"What was that?"

"Hell, I don't know."

"Jake, let's go back down. Please." Her greatest fear was walking into a bat's nest or something worse.

"We already went over that. The light's got to be around here someplace."

"Sure, and in the meantime we don't know..."

"Damn."

Lily's hand tightened around his, her fingers clammy. "Now what's wrong?"

"My knee bumped into something."

"That does it. We're going back." Jake could stay up here if he wanted, but she was leaving. From the minute they'd stepped inside this tomb, Lily had felt uneasy.

"Lily," he argued.

Jerking her hand free, she turned toward the stairs and the faint beam of light. It looked as though the attic door had eased shut, cutting off what little illumination there had been from the hall. Everything was terribly dark and spooky. "I'm getting out of here," she declared, unable to keep the catch out of her voice. "This place is giving me the heebie-jeebies." More interested in making her escape than being cautious, Lily turned away and walked straight into a spider's web. A disgusted sound slid from her throat as her hands flew up to free her face from the fine, sticky threads. A prickling fear shot up her spine as she felt something scamper across her foot.

Her heart rammed against her breast like a jackhammer as the terror gripped her and she let out a bloodcurdling cry. "Jake...Jake."

He was with her in seconds, roughly pulling her into his arms. "What the hell?"

She clung to him, frantically wrapping her arms around his neck. Her face was buried in his shoulder as she trembled with fear. His arms around her waist half lifted her from the floor. "Lily, you're all right," he whispered frantically. His hold, secure and warm, drove out the terror. "I've got you," he added.

It took all the strength she could muster just to nod.

Jake's hand brushed the wispy curls from her temple. "Lily," he repeated soothingly. "I told you I'd protect you." His warm breath fanned her face, creating an entirely new set of sensations. His scent, a combination of sweat and man, was unbelievably intoxicating. For the first time Lily became aware of how tightly pressed her body was to the rock hardness of his. Her grip slackened and she slid intimately down the length of him until her feet touched the floor. The hem of her blouse rode up, exposing her midriff so that her bare skin rubbed against the muscular wall of his chest. His hands found their place in the small of her back and seemed to hold her there, pressing her all the closer. Her breasts were flattened to his upper torso and her nerves fired to life at the merest brush of his body.

As if hypnotized, their eyes met and held in the faint light. It was as though they were seeing each other for the first time. Her pulse fluttered wildly at his look of curious surprise as his gaze lowered to her mouth.

"Jake?" Her voice was the faintest whisper, wavering and unsure.

His eyes darkened and a thick frown formed on his face. Slowly, almost as if drawn by something other than his will, Jake lowered his mouth to hers. Warm lips met warm lips in an exploratory kiss that was as gentle as it was unhurried. Trembling, her mouth stroked his and his hands tightened painfully around her waist.

"Lily." His mouth left the sweetness of hers and sounded oddly raspy and unsure. Her eyes remained tightly closed to shut out reality.

"That shouldn't have happened." Somehow she had found her voice.

"Do you want an apology?"

Her arms slid from around his neck and fell to her side as he released her. "No..." she whispered. "I should be the one to apologize...I don't know what came over me."

"You're right about this place," he admitted on a harsh note. "There is something spooky about it. Let's get out of here."

By the time they'd returned to the living room, Lily had regained her equilibrium and could smile over the peculiar events in the attic.

"What's so damn amusing?" He didn't sound the least bit pleased by their adventure, and stalked ahead of her, sitting in the fan-back bamboo chair usually reserved for Gram.

"Honestly, Jake, can you imagine *us kissing*?"

"We just did," he reminded her soberly, his voice firm as his watchful eyes studied her. "And if we're both smart, we'll forget it ever happened."

Lily sat on the sofa, tucking her legs under her. "I suppose you're right. It's just that after being such good friends for the past year, it was a shock. Elaine would never forgive me."

"Would you lay off Elaine? I've told you a thousand times that it's been over for months." Jake grimaced at the sound of the other woman's name. His relationship with Elaine Wittenberg had developed nicely in the beginning. She was impressed with his writing, encouraging even. Then bit by bit, with intrusive politeness, Elaine had started to reorganize his life. First came the suggestion that he change jobs. Driving a cab didn't pay that well, and with his talents he could do anything. She started introducing him to her friends, making contacts for him. The problem was that Jake liked his life exactly the way it was. Elaine had been a close call—too close. Jake had come within inches of waking up one morning living in a three-bedroom house with a white picket fence and a new car parked in the garage—a house and a car with big monthly payments. True, Lily was just as eager for the same material possessions, but at least she was honest about it.

"Well, you needn't worry," Lily told him, taking a deep breath and releasing it slowly. "Just because we kissed, it doesn't mean anything."

Her cold logic irritated him. "Let's not talk about it, all right? It was a mistake and it's over."

Lily arched a delicate brow and shrugged one shoulder. "Fine." His attitude didn't please her in the least. As far as she knew, Jake wasn't one to sweep things under the carpet and forget they existed. If anything, he faced life head-on.

Abruptly getting to his feet, Jake stalked to the other side of the living room. Confused, Lily watched the impatient, angry way he moved. "I'll see you tomorrow," he said on his way to the front door.

"Okay."

The door slammed closed and Lily didn't move. What an incredibly strange night it had been. First, the golden opportunity of finding that crazy song for the Texan. Then, wilder still was Jake's kissing her in the attic. Even now she could feel the pressure of his mouth on hers, and the salty-sweet taste of him lingered on her lips. He'd held her close and the musky scent of his maleness had been heightened by the stuffy air of the attic.

But, Lily realized with a start, the kiss had been a moment out of time and was never meant to be. Jake was right. They should simply put it out of their minds and forget it had ever happened. A single kiss should be no threat to a year of solid friendship. They knew each other too well to get caught up in a romantic relationship. Lily had seen the type of woman Jake appreciated, and she wasn't even close to it. Jake's idea of a wonderful woman was Mother Theresa, Bo Derek and Betty Crocker all rolled into one perfect female specimen. Conversely, her idea of the ideal man was J. Paul Getty, John Wayne and Mr. Goodwrench. No... Jake and she would always be friends; they'd make terrible lovers....

The next morning when Lily found her way into the kitchen, Gram was already up and about. Her bright-red hair was tightly curled into a hundred ringlets and held in place with bobby pins.

"Morning," Lily mumbled and pulled out a kitchen chair, eager to speak to her grandmother.

Gram didn't acknowledge the greeting. Instead, the older woman concentrated on opening a variety of bottles, extracting her daily quota of pills.

Lily waited until her grandmother had finished swallowing the thirteen garlic tablets and a number of vitamins, and had chewed the six blanched almonds.

This daily ritual was Gram's protection from cancer. The world could scoff, but at seventy-four Gram was as fit as someone twenty years her junior.

"I didn't hear you come in last night."

A faint smile played at the edges of Lily's soft mouth. "I know. Gram, have you ever heard of the song 'Santa Fe Gal of Mine'?"

The older woman's look was thoughtful and Lily nibbled nervously on her bottom lip. "It's been a lotta years since I heard that ol' song."

"You remember it?" Relief washed through Lily until she sagged against the back of the chair, weak with appreciation. If anyone could tell her about that song, it had to be Gram. Lily marveled again at her grandmother's memory.

"Play a few bars for me, girl."

Lily tensed and the silence stretched until her nerve endings screamed with it. "I don't know the song, Gram. I thought *you* did."

"I do," she insisted, shaking her bright red head. "I don't remember it offhand, is all."

Is all, Lily repeated mentally in a panic. "When do you think you'll remember it?"

"I can't rightly say. Give me a day or two."

A day or two! "Gram, I haven't got that long. Our future could depend on 'Santa Fe Gal of Mine.' Think."

Stirring the peanut butter with a knife, Gram picked up a soda cracker and dabbed a layer of chunky-style spread across the top before popping it into her mouth.

Lily wanted to scream that this wasn't a time for food, but she pressed her lips tightly shut, forcing down the panic. Gram didn't do well under pressure.

"What do you want to know for?" Gram asked after a good five minutes had elapsed. Meanwhile, she'd eaten six soda crackers, each loaded with a thick layer of peanut butter.

"A rich man requested that song last night. A very rich man who had a generous look about him," Lily explained, doing her best to keep the excitement out of her voice. "If I can come up with that song, he'd be happy. And Gram, he looked like the type who would show his appreciation."

"We could use a little appreciation, couldn't we, girl?"

"Oh, Gram, you know we could."

"If I can't think of it, Gene Autry would know." Gram often spoke as if famous personalities were her lifelong friends and all she had to do was pick up the phone and give a jingle.

"Did Gene Autry sing the original version?"

"Now that you mention it, he might have been the one," she said, scratching the side of her head.

Lily perked up. Gram had every record Gene Autry had ever sung. "Then you have it."

"I must," she agreed. "Someplace."

"Someplace" turned out to be in the furnace room in the basement five hours later. The next few hours were spent transposing the scratchy old record into notes Lily could play on the piano.

When she sat at the grand piano at five that evening in the Wheaton lobby, 'Santa Fe Gal of Mine' was forever embedded in her brain. Each note had been agonized over. There couldn't be a worse way to memorize a song. Lily had never been able to play very well by ear.

As it worked out, the timing had been tight and consequently Lily had been unable to pay the amount of attention she would have liked to her dress and makeup.

The lobby was busy with people strolling in and out, registering for a wholesale managers' conference. At the moment the only thing Lily was interested in was one Texan with a love for an ol' Gene Autry number.

During the evening, Lily twice played the song she had come to hate more than any of the others. Her only reward was a few disgruntled stares. The lively Western piece wasn't the "elevator" style she'd been hired to play. The second go-around with 'Santa Fe Gal' and Lily caught the manager giving her a look of displeasure. Instantly, Lily switched over to something he'd consider more appropriate: 'Moon River.'

As the evening progressed, Lily's plastic smile became more and more forced. She'd gone to all this trouble for nothing. Her stomach felt as if it were weighted with a lead balloon. All the hassle she'd gone through, all the work, had been for nothing. Gram would be so disappointed. Hell, Gram nothing. Lily felt like crying.

As usual, Jake was waiting for her outside the hotel.

"How'd it go?" he asked as she approached the cab. One look at her sorrowful dark eyes and Jake climbed out of the cab. "What happened?"

"Nothing." Even the one word had difficulty making it out with the hard lump constricting her throat.

"J. Paul Getty wasn't the appreciative type?"

She shook her head, half expecting Jake to scold her for being so incredibly naive. "No."

"What, then?"

"He didn't show."

Jake held open the taxi door for her. "Oh, Lily, I'm sorry."

"It's not your fault," she returned loyally. "I was the stupid one. I can't believe that I could have gotten so excited over an overweight Texan who wanted to hear a crummy song that's older than I am."

"But he was a rich Texan."

"Probably into oil or gold."

"Probably," Jake repeated sympathetically.

Jake had walked around the front of the taxi when the captain of the bellboys came hurrying out of the hotel. "Miss Lily!" he called, flagging her down. "Someone left a message for you."

Chapter Two

A message?'' Lily's gaze clashed with Jake's as excitement welled up inside her, lifting the dark shroud of depression that had settled over her earlier.

"Thanks, Henry.'' Lily gave the hotel's senior bellhop a brilliant smile. Two minutes before, Lily would never have believed that something as simple as an envelope could chase the clouds of doubt from her heart.

"Well, what does it say?'' Jake questioned, leaning through the open car window. He appeared as anxious as Lily.

"Give me a minute to open it, for heaven's sake.'' She ripped apart the beige envelope bearing the Wheaton's logo. Her gaze flew over the bold penstrokes, reading as fast as she could. "It's him.''

"Daddy Warbucks?''

"Yes,'' she repeated, her voice quavering with anticipation. "Only his real name is Rex Flanders. He says he got hung up in a meeting and couldn't make it downstairs, but he wanted me to know he heard the song and it was just as good as he remembered. He wants to thank me." Searching for something more, Lily turned over the single sheet, thinking she must have missed or dropped it in her hastiness. Surely he meant that he wanted to thank her with more than a simple message. The least she'd expected was a dinner invitation. With hurried, anxious movements she checked her lap, scrambling to locate the envelope she'd so carelessly discarded only a moment before.

"What are you looking for?" Jake asked, perplexed.

"Nothing." Defeat caused her voice to drop half an octave. Lily couldn't take her eyes from the few scribbled lines on the single sheet of hotel stationery. Shaking her head, she hoped to clear her muddled thoughts. She'd been stupid to expect anything more than a simple thank-you. Rich men always had women chasing after them. There wasn't one thing that would make her stand out in a crowd. She wasn't strikingly beautiful, or talented, or even sophisticated. Little about her would make her attractive to a wealthy man.

"Lily?" Gently, Jake placed a hand on her forearm. His tender touch warmed her cool skin and brought feeling back to her numb fingers. "What's wrong?"

A tremulous smile briefly touched her lips. "Me. I'm wrong. Oh, Jake, I'm never going to find a rich man who'll want to marry me. And even if I was lucky enough to interest someone in me, they'd take one look at Gram and Herbie and start running in the opposite direction."

"I don't see why," he contradicted sharply. "I didn't."

"Yeah, but you're just as weird as we are."

"Thanks." The bitter taste of sarcasm coated his tongue. So Lily thought he was as eccentric as her grandmother. All right, he'd agree that he didn't show the corporate ambitions that drove so many of his college friends. He liked his life. He was perfectly content to live on a sailboat for the remainder of his days, without a care or responsibility. There wasn't anything in this world that he couldn't walk away from, and that was exactly the way he wanted it. No complications. No one to answer to. And best of all—no women. Except Gram and Lily. But even now his platonic relationship with Lily was beginning to cause problems. He admired Lily. What he liked best about her was that she had no designs on his heart and no desire to change him. She was an honest, forthright woman. She knew what she wanted and made no bones about it. Their kiss of the day before had been a fluke that wouldn't happen again. He'd make sure of that.

"I didn't mean that the way it sounded," Lily mumbled her apology. "You're the best friend I've got. I'm feeling a bit defeated at the moment. Tomorrow I'll be back to my normal self again."

Silently walking around the front of the taxi, Jake climbed into the driver's seat and started the engine with a flick of his wrist. "I can't say I blame you." And he didn't. After everything she'd gone through getting the music for that Texan's song, she had every right to be disappointed.

"It's me I'm angry with," Lily said, breaking the silence. "I shouldn't have put such stock in a simple request."

Jake blamed himself. He should have cautioned her, but at the time he'd been so surprised that he hadn't known what he was feeling—maybe even a bit of jealousy, which had shocked the hell out of him. Later he'd discarded that notion. He wanted Lily to be as happy as she deserved, but there was something about this Texan that had troubled him from the beginning.

The moment Lily had mentioned she'd met someone, warning lights had gone off inside his head. His protective instinct, for some reason he couldn't put into words, had been aroused. That alien impulse had been the cause of the incident in the attic. He didn't honestly regret kissing Lily, but it was just that type of thing that could ruin a good friendship. The Texan meant trouble for Lily. Jake knew it as strongly as if there were neon lights flashing the message. Rarely had he felt anything more potently. It'd taken him half the night to realize that the paunchy Texan was what bothered him. Now, after Lily's revelation, Jake could afford to be generous.

"How about if we go fishing tomorrow?"

Lily straightened, her dark eyes glowing with pleasure at the invitation. "On the boat?" Over the past year, Jake had only taken her out on the sloop for short, limited periods of time. Lily loved sailing and was convinced that the man she married would have to own a sail boat.

"With Gram," he insisted, granting her a rare smile that curved his mouth sensuously upward. "We'll make a day of it, pack a bottle of good wine, some cheese and a loaf of freshly baked French bread, and beer with cheese and crackers for me.''

"Jake, that sounds wonderful.'' Already her heart was lifting with anticipation. Only Jake would know that an entire day on his sailboat would cheer her like this.

"We deserve a one-day vacation from all our ills. I'll park the cab, pack away the typewriter and take you to places you have never been.''

Lily expelled a deep sigh of contentment. "It sounds great, but Thursday's Gram's bingo day. Nothing will convince her to give that up.''

A faint smile sparked from Jake's cool jade eyes. Lily's grandmother had her own get-rich schemes going. "Then it'll have to be the two of us. Are you still game?''

"You bet.'' Lily closed her eyes, picturing the brisk wind whipping her hair freely about her face as the boat sliced through the deep-green waters of San Francisco Bay.

Within ten hours, the daydream had become reality. The wind carried Lily's low laugh as she tossed back her head and the warm breeze ruffled her thick, unbound hair. The boat keeled sharply and cut a deep path through the choppy water. Lily had climbed to the front of the boat to raise the sails and was now sitting on the bow, luxuriating in sensations of power and freedom she found nearly overwhelming. She wanted to capture this utopian state of being and hug it to her breast forever. She didn't dare turn back and let Jake see her. He'd laugh at her childish spirit and tease her unmercifully. Lily wanted nothing to ruin the magnificent day.

For the first hour of their trip, Lily remained forward while Jake manned the helm. Keeping his mind to the task was difficult. He couldn't ever remember seeing Lily so carefree and happy. She was a natural sailor. He'd taken other women aboard *Lucky Lady* and always regretted it. Elaine, for one. In the beginning, she'd pretended to love his boat as much as he, but Jake hadn't been fooled. Elaine's big mistake had come when she suggested that he move off the boat and into an apartment. Pitted against his only true love, Jake decided to keep *Lady* and dump Elaine. And not a moment since had he regretted the decision.

Watching Lily produced a curious sense of pride in Jake. Laughing, she turned back and shouted something to him. The wind whirled her voice away and he hadn't a clue as to what she'd said, but the exhilaration in her flushed face wasn't something that could be manufactured. It surprised Jake how much he enjoyed watching her. She reminded him of the sea nymphs sailors of old claimed inhabited the waters.

As he watched her, Jake realized that Lily was his friend and they were fortunate to share a special kind of relationship. But it wasn't until that moment that Jake noticed just how beautiful she was. In the year he'd known her, Lily's youthful features had filled out with vivid promise. Her long hair was a rich, dark shade of mahogany and he'd rarely seen it unbound. That day, instead of piling it on top of her head the way she normally did, Lily had left it free so that it fell in gentle waves around her shoulders. Her natural gracefulness was what struck Jake most. Her walk was decidedly provocative. Jake smiled to himself with an inner pride at the interest Lily's gently rounded hips generated from the opposite sex. If that Texan had seen her walk he would have sent her far more than a simple message. But what Jake loved mainly about Lily was her eyes. Never in his life had he met anyone with eyes so dark and expressive. Some days they were like cellophane and he could read her moods as clearly as the words in a book. He could imagine what it would be like making love to her. He wouldn't need to see anything but her eyes to...

Abruptly he shook himself and severed the disturbing thoughts. His fingers tightened around the helm and he looked sharply out to sea. Hell, what was the matter with him? He was looking at Lily as a prospective lover.

"How about a cup of coffee?" Lily called, standing beside the mast. The wind whipped her hair behind her like a magnificent flag and Jake sucked in his breath at the alluring picture she made.

"I'll get it," he shouted. "Take over here for me, will you?"

A quick, tantalizing smile spread across her vivid features as she nodded and hurried down to join him at the helm. She laughed as he gave her careful instructions. She didn't need them. She felt giddy and reckless and wonderful.

Turning away, it was all Jake could do not to kiss her again. Mumbling under his breath, he descended to the galley and sleeping area of the boat.

Lily didn't know what was troubling Jake. She'd witnessed the dark scowl on his face and been surprised. He returned a few minutes later with two steaming mugs, handing her one.

"Is something wrong?" she ventured.

"Nothing," he answered sharply, keeping his gaze from lingering on her soft, unconsciously inviting mouth.

"You look like you want to bite off my head again."

"Again?" Jake was stalling for time. This foul mood was Lily's fault. She didn't know what she was doing to him, and that was his problem.

"Yes, again," she repeated. "Like you did the other night when I told you about Rex."

"I've been doing some thinking about that ungrateful Texan," he said with a brooding, thoughtful look that narrowed his eyes and tightened his jaw. "There's something about him I don't trust."

"But you've never seen him," Lily countered, confused.

"I didn't have to. Just hearing about him was enough. I don't want you to see him again."

"Jake!"

"I mean it, Lily."

Astonished, Lily sat with her jaw sagging and turned away from him, cupping the steaming mug with both hands. Jake had never asked her to do anything. It wasn't like him to suddenly order her about and make demands. She swallowed her indignation. "Will you give me a reason?"

Drawing in a deep, irritated breath, Jake looked out over the green water and wondered at his own high-handedness. The Texan had been bothering him for two days. He hadn't wanted to say anything and even now, he wasn't entirely convinced he was doing the right thing. "It's a gut feeling I have. My instincts got me out of 'Nam alive. I can't explain it, Lily, but I'm asking you to trust me in this."

"All right," she agreed, somewhat deflated. At the rate things were progressing with Rex What's-his-name, she wouldn't have the opportunity to see him again anyway. In reality, Jake wasn't asking much. He was her friend and she trusted his judgment, albeit at the moment reluctantly.

"Someone else will come along," Jake assured her, and a lazy grin crept across his tanned face. "If not, you'll trap one as effectively as the fish we're about to lure to our dinner plates."

"You make it sound too easy." He wasn't the one who sat at that piano night after night playing those same songs again and again and again.

"It is." He handed her a fishing pole and carefully revealed to her the finer points of casting. Luckily, Lily was a fast learner and he took pains not to touch her. Shaking off his mood, he gave her a friendly smile. "Before you know it, our meal will mosey along," he said with a distinct Southern drawl. "And who knows? It could be an oil-rich Texan bass."

Lily laughed, enjoying their light banter.

"Every woman scheming to marry money has to keep her eye out for a tightfisted shark, but then again—" he paused for emphasis "—you might stumble upon a flounder in commodities."

"A generous flounder," Lily added.

"Naturally." Cupping his hand behind his head, Jake leaned back, crossed his long legs at the ankle and closed his eyes. He felt better. He hadn't a clue why he felt so strongly about that rich Texan. He just sensed trouble.

* * *

"There's another message for you, Miss Lily," Henry informed her when she arrived at the hotel the following evening.

Lily stared at the envelope as if it were a snake about to lash out at her. "A message?" she repeated, her voice sounding amazingly like an echo.

"From the same man as before," Henry explained with ageless, questioning eyes.

Undoubtedly the elderly bellboy couldn't understand her reluctance now when only the day before she behaved as if she'd won the Irish sweepstakes.

"Thank you." Lily took the folded note and made her way into the grand lobby. The manager acknowledged her with a faint nod, but Lily's answering smile was forced. The message lay on the keyboard of the piano for several moments before she had the courage to open it.

Hello, Lily—the bellhop told me your name. He also told me what time you'd be in today. I've thought about you and your music. I'm hoping that a sweet filly like you won't think it too forward of me to suggest we meet later for a drink.
                                            Rex Flanders

A drink...surely that would be harmless, especially if they stayed right here in the hotel. Jake wouldn't care. Her hands moved to the ivory keys and automatically began the repertoire of songs that was only a step above the canned music that played in the elevators.

Although her fingers moved with practiced ease, Lily's thoughts were in turmoil. She'd promised Jake she wouldn't see Rex again. And she'd agreed. At the time it had seemed such a little thing. The way the contact with Rex had developed after she'd found the song, it hadn't seemed likely she'd have the chance to see him again. Now she deeply regretted having consented to Jake's request so readily. This was her first chance in months. Months! Her big break had arrived and she was going to have to refuse probably the richest man she'd ever met. And all because Jake had some stupid *feeling*. It wasn't fair. Jake hadn't even seen Rex. How could anyone have a feeling about someone they hadn't even met?

Later, when she had a moment, Lily penned a note to Rex, declining his invitation. She didn't offer an excuse. It'd sound ludicrous to explain that a friend had warned her against him. *You see, my friend, Jake, has the instincts of Rambo and he claims you're bad news for me. He felt so strongly about it that he made me promise I wouldn't see you again.* Rex would laugh himself all the way home to Texas. No one in their right mind would blame him.

Jake was out front, standing beside his taxi when she appeared. He waited for her nearly every night and gave her a free ride home. Tonight she felt like taking the bus, but one look at the darkening sky convinced her otherwise. The night was overcast, with thick gray clouds rolling in over the bay and adding a shroud of gloom to the picturesque city on its shores. Lily didn't need the weather to dampen her already foul mood.

"I hope you're happy," she announced tersely and opened the car door.

"Relatively. What's your problem?"

"At the moment, you."

Their gazes met, a clash of befuddled emerald and blazing jet. Lily had been waiting for months for this opportunity—months when she'd built up fanciful dreams—months when she'd schemed and planned for exactly this moment. And now, because of Jake, she was walking away from the opportunity of a lifetime.

"Me!" Jake cocked his head to one side, studying her as his gaze narrowed thoughtfully. "What do you mean?" His tone told her clearly that he didn't appreciate being put on the defensive.

"Rex asked me out."

"And you refused?" Instinctively he felt the hard muscles of his shoulders tense. So Daddy Warbucks was back. Somehow Jake had known the man would return.

"I'm here, aren't I? But I'll have you know that I regret that damn promise and would take it back in a minute if you'd let me." She eyed him hopefully, but at the sight of the deep grooves that were forming at the sides of his mouth, Lily could tell he wouldn't relent.

Jake was conscious of an odd sensation surging through his blood. He'd experienced it only a few times in his life and always when something monumental was about to happen. The first time had been as an eight-year-old kid. He'd been lost in the downtown area at Christmastime and frightened half out of his wits. The huge skyscrapers had seemed to close in around him until he could taste the panic. Then, the feeling had come and he'd stopped, looked around, got his bearing and found his way home on his own, astonishing his mother. Later, in high school, the same feeling had come before he was scheduled to play in a football game in which he scored three touchdowns

and became a school hero. Again he'd felt that peculiar sensation in the dense jungles of Vietnam and it
had saved his life. Jake had never told anyone about
these feelings. Words couldn't adequately describe
them; they were too complex to define.

"No," he said with cold deliberation. "I'm not
changing my mind."

"Jake," she moaned, feeling wretched.

"I'm asking you to trust me." He said it without
looking at her, not wanting her to see the intensity of
his determination. His fists were clenched so tightly at
his sides that his fingers ached. Lily could bat her long
eyelashes at him all she wanted and it wouldn't change
how he felt. Hell, he wished she'd find her J. Paul
Getty and get married if that was what she wanted so
badly. But this Texan wasn't the right man for Lily.

Without further discussion, Lily slid inside the cab.
Disappointment caused her shoulders to droop and
her head to hang so low that her chin rested against the
bright-red collar of her sequined gown. She was more
tired than she could remember having been in a long
time. Of all the men in the world, she trusted Jake the
most. More than her father. But then it was difficult
to have too much confidence in a vague childhood
memory. Lily's father had died when she was twelve,
but she had trouble picturing him in her mind. As far
as Lily could recall, she'd only seen her father a
handful of times. In some ways Lily wished she didn't
trust Jake so much; it would make things a whole lot
easier.

Jake closed her door, his hands gripping the open
window as he watched her through weary eyes. For
half a second, he toyed with the idea of releasing her

from the promise. But he entertained the idea only fleetingly. He knew better.

"Can you take me home now?"

"Sure." He hurried around the cab and climbed into the front seat beside her. A flick of the key and the engine gave the gentle purr of a well-tuned vehicle. "You won't regret this," Jake said, flashing her one of his most brilliant smiles.

Lily's look was deadpan. "I regret it already," she said and stared out the side window.

Those thoughtless words hounded Lily the remainder of the evening. Jake was her friend—her best friend—and she was treating him like the tax man. Usually, at the end of the evening Jake would stop by the house on his way back to the dock where his sailboat was moored. But he didn't show up, although Lily waited up half the night. She didn't blame him. They'd hardly said a word on the way home and when he pulled to the curb in front of Gram's rickety old house, Lily had practically jumped out of the taxi. She hadn't even bothered to say good-night.

The following morning Lily was wakened by Gram singing an African chant. Tossing aside the covers, Lily leaped from the bed and rushed into the kitchen. Gram only sang in Swahili during the good times.

"Gram, what happened?" she asked excitedly, rubbing the sleep from her eyes. Two steps into the large central kitchen and Lily discovered Gram clothed in full African dress. Yard upon yard of bold chartreuse printed material was draped around her waist with deep folds falling halfway to the floor. The shirt was made of matching material and hung from her shoulders, draping into large bell sleeves. Wisps of bright-red hair escaped the chartreuse turban that was wrapped around her head. Ten thin gold bracelets dangled like charms from each wrist.

"Gram." Lily stopped cold, not knowing what to make of this apparition.

The older woman made a dignified bow and hugged Lily fiercely. *"Nzuri sana,"* she greeted her, ceremoniously kissing her granddaughter on the cheek.

Lily was too bemused to react. *"Nzuri sana,"* she returned, slowly sinking into a kitchen chair. Her grandmother might behave a bit oddly on occasion, but nothing like this.

Continuing to chant in low tones, Gram turned and pulled a fifty-dollar bill from the folds of her outfit and waved it under Lily's nose.

"Gram, where did you get that?" All kinds of anxious thoughts were going through her mind. Maybe Gram was so worried over their finances that she'd done something illegal.

Hips swaying, Gram crossed the room and chuckled. The unmusical sound echoed against the walls. "Bingo," she cried, and removed four more fifty-dollar bills.

"You won at bingo!" Lily cried, jumping up from the chair and dancing around the room. Their arms circled each other's waists and they skipped around the kitchen like schoolgirls until Lily was breathless and dizzy.

"You buy yourself something special," Gram insisted when they'd settled down. "Something alluring so those rich men at the Wheaton won't be able to take their eyes off you."

Lily did her utmost to comply. She left the house and spent the rest of the morning shopping. Half the day was gone by the time she'd located the perfect outfit. It was a silky black dress with a Ribbonette bodice that veed provocatively in the front, granting a glimpse of cleavage and hinting at the swelling fullness of her breasts. Studying herself in the mirror, Lily turned sideways, one hand on her hips, and rested her chin on her shoulder as she pouted her lips. Heavens, she couldn't tell if she would send someone into rapture over her natural beauty or be arrested for misrepresentation.

After paying for the dress, Lily hurried home. She rushed up to her bedroom and donned her new purchase. Doubtfully she eyed her reflection in the mirror. Jake would tell her if the dress had the desired effect. Besides, she owed him an apology.

The ride to the marina was just as hectic. Jake just had to be there.

His boat was in the slip at the marina when she approached. Lily had never visited him without an invitation and felt uneasy about doing so now.

"Jake," she called from the dock. "Are you there?" The boards rolled slightly under her high heels and Lily had to brace herself. "Jake," she repeated louder, hugging the full-length coat close to her.

"Coming." His tone sounded irritated and he was frowning as he stuck his head out from below deck. He stopped when he saw it was Lily and smoothed a hand through his thick hair. "Hi." Slowly he came topside. "What are you doing here? And why in heaven's name are you wearing that ridiculous coat?"

Lily glanced down over the long wool garment that had once belonged to Gram and felt all the more silly. "Gram won two hundred and fifty dollars at bingo last night. I bought a new dress and want you to tell me if I look all right. Can I come aboard?"

"Sure." Jake didn't sound nearly as eager as she'd hoped he would.

"What do you think about this dress?" she asked. "Be honest, now." She lifted the gray wool coat from her shoulders and let it slip down her arms. One glance at Lily in that beautiful dress, and Jake could barely take his eyes off her. She looked sensational—a knockout.

"I...I didn't know if you'd want to see me."

"Why wouldn't I?" His answer was guarded, his words quiet. Still he couldn't take his eyes from her.

"I feel terrible about yesterday."

"No problem." He reached out his hand in silent invitation for her to join him and Lily deftly crossed the rough wooden dock to his polished deck.

"Gram insisted I buy something new. How do you like it?"

"I like it fine," he murmured, doing his best to look away. "You look great, actually." That had to be the understatement of the century.

"Do you honestly think so?" she asked excitedly. "I'm telling you, Jake, I don't know if I look sexy or if I look like I'm coming down with a bad case of mono."

Jake chuckled. "I'd venture it was safe to say that you look nice."

"What a good friend you are, Jake," she answered softly. "Thank you."

"Think nothing of it." With a sweep of his arm, he invited her below. "Do you want a cup of coffee?"

"Thanks." She paused to remove her shoes and handed them to Jake. "Would you put these some-place where I won't forget them?"

"Sure." He went down before her and waited at the base of the steps in case she needed help. One bare foot appeared on the top rung of the ladder and the side split in the skirt revealed the ivory skin of her thigh as the next foot descended. Jake felt his heart constrict. No one should be allowed to have skin that lovely. It looked as smooth as silk and as pale as alabaster. He sighed with relief as she reached the bottom rung and turned around, eyes sparkling, to face him.

"I'll get you a cup," he announced, disliking the close confines of his cabin for the first time. Lily seemed to fill up every inch of available space, looming over him with that alluring scent that belonged only to her.

"How's the writing going?"

"Good." It wasn't. Actually he'd faced writer's block all day, and determined that it was Lily's fault. He didn't like what was happening between them and yet seemed powerless to stop it.

"Heard any more from Daddy Warbucks?"

"No." Lily slid into the tight booth that served as the kitchen table. "I won't see him again," she told him with dark, serious eyes. "I promised you I wouldn't."

"Someone else will come along." And soon, he hoped. The quicker Lily found herself a sugar daddy, the better it would be for him.

"I know." She smiled up at him briefly as he set the mug on the table.

He didn't join her, fearing that if he slid into the seat beside her, they might accidentally brush against one another. And touching Lily wearing that dress frightened Jake. It would be the attic all over again and he knew he wouldn't be able to stop himself. As it was now, he could barely tear his eyes from her. She lifted her mug and blew against the edge before taking a sip. Her dewy lips drew his gaze like a magnet. Jake turned around and added some sugar to his coffee.

"I didn't know you used sugar."

"I don't," he said, turning back to her.

"You just dumped three tablespoons into your cup." She sounded as perplexed as he felt.

Jake lifted one shoulder in a halfhearted shrug. "It must be something in the air."

"Must be," Lily agreed, not knowing what he was talking about. She dropped her gaze to the dark, steaming liquid. "I've been thinking that I need lessons on how to flirt." Jake nearly choked on his coffee and did an admirable job of containing himself. Lily was so unconsciously alluring, that he couldn't believe that any man could ignore her.

"Will you teach me, Jake?" There wasn't anyone she trusted more. Jake had been all over the world and done everything she hadn't. Lily didn't think there was a thing he didn't know. "You'd be perfect."

With that, he did choke on a mouthful of coffee. "Me?"

"Yes, you."

"Lily, come on. I don't know anything about feminine stuff like that."

"Sure you do," she contradicted, warming to her subject. "Every time I bat my eyelashes at a man, I'm convinced he thinks I've got a nerve disease."

"Ask Gram."

"I can't do that." She waved her hand dismissively. "Just tell me what Elaine looked like that made you go all weak inside."

"Hell, I don't know."

"Like this?" She dropped her eyes and parted her lips, giving him her most sultry look.

Jake experienced a savage tenderness unlike anything he'd ever known. He couldn't teach her to flirt. She was a natural. "Something like that," he murmured at last.

Discouraged, Lily straightened. Elaine had known exactly what to do to make a man notice her. For months, Jake had been so crazy over the other woman that he'd hardly ever come by for a visit. It had shocked Lily when they'd split. Maybe Jake wasn't the best person to teach her what she needed to know. But she knew he wasn't immune to a woman's wiles. The problem was he thought of her as a sister. She could probably turn up on his dock naked and he'd barely notice.

"Forget it," she mumbled. "I'll ask Gram."

Chapter Three

Jake paced the small confines of his galley like a man trapped in an obligatory telephone conversation. He had to do something, and fast. Roughly he combed his fingers through his hair and caught his breath. Lily was beginning to look good to him. Damn good. And that was trouble with a capital *T*. Either he found himself a woman, and quick, or…or he'd take it upon himself to find Lily a wealthy man. Both appeared formidable tasks.

If he involved himself with a woman, it would surely end in disaster. No woman would be satisfied with his carefree life-style. Oh, no. Far be it for a woman to see a man happy. It was in their blood to shackle a man and bind him with obligations and responsibilities. Every woman he'd known, with the exception of Lily, had taken it upon herself to "save" him. The problem was, Jake didn't want to be redeemed by a woman's ambitions.

But locating a rich man for Lily wouldn't be easy. It wasn't as if he traveled in elite circles. He had a few contacts—buddies from school—but no one like the wealthy type Lily wanted.

There was Rick, his friend from college days. From everything Jake had heard, Rick had done well for himself and was living in San Francisco. It wouldn't hurt to look up Rick and see if he was still single. Jake didn't like the idea, but it couldn't be helped.

Humming softly, Lily smiled at the doorman at the Wheaton and sauntered into the posh hotel as if she owned it. She was practicing for the time when she could enter a public place and cause faces to turn and whispers to fill the air. She'd ignore them, of course, and point her nose toward the ceiling, pretending not to notice. A grand entrance, however, required diamonds and furs and she had neither. Not yet, anyway.

Lily felt good. The meeting with Jake hadn't turned out to be the confrontation she'd expected. Jake had had every reason to be angry with her, and wasn't. If anything he'd behaved a bit weirdly. He'd seemed to go out of his way not to be close to her. When she was on one side of the boat, he'd stand on the other. Another thing he'd done was avoid eye contact as though he were guilty of something. But, then again, what didn't she know about bizarre? She'd grown up with the eccentric and the unconventional. She and Gram might lack the finer things in life, but they certainly had never been bored.

A large bouquet of red roses on the piano was a mild surprise. Flowers weren't something the Wheaton's manager would willingly approve for her. A small white envelope propped against the ivory keys caused her eyes to widen, and her heart to do a tiny flip-flop. Lily knew without looking that Rex had sent the flowers. Her hands trembled noticeably as she removed the card and read the bold handwriting: *Sorry you couldn't make it, little filly. I'll see you next month on the 25th at nine.*

Lily swallowed a nervous lump that clogged her throat. Next month or next year; it wouldn't make any difference. She'd given Jake her word and she wouldn't go back on it no matter how tempting. And tempting it was. Rex was interested. He must be, to send her the flowers and ask her out again.

With a heavy heart, Lily pulled out the piano bench and sat, poising her hands over the pearly keys and closing her ears to the same old songs.

As usual, Jake was waiting for her at the end of her shift. His gaze focused on the roses and narrowed fractionally.

"Daddy Warbucks?"

"Yeah." Lily didn't know why she felt so guilty, but she did. This was the first time in her life that anyone had sent her roses and she wasn't about to leave them at the Wheaton. "He's gone."

Jake felt a surge of relief wash over him. He wished like the dickens that he had felt differently about that Texan. If he had, it would have been the end of his troubles. Lily could have had her rich man and he could go about his life without complications.

"He left a note with the roses, asking me out next month. Apparently he'll be back in town then."

"Are you going?"

The muscles at the side of her mouth ached as Lily compressed her lips into a tight line. "No."

"Good."

Maybe it was good for Jake, but Lily was miserable. "Will I see you later?" she asked when he dropped her off in front of Gram's house.

"I'll be by."

Even with all his hang-ups about personal freedom and restricting schedules, Lily knew that if Jake said he'd be someplace, he'd be there eventually. Purposely waiting up for him, she sat watching the late-late show dressed in a worn terry-cloth housecoat that was tightly cinched at the waist. In an effort to stay awake, she sipped Marmite, a yeast extract, which had been stirred into hot water. Years ago while traveling in New Zealand, Gram had had her first taste of the thick, chocolate-like substance and had grown to love it. She received the product on a regular basis from family friends now and spread it lightly over her morning toast. Lily preferred the dark extract diluted.

The movie was an old Gary Cooper one that had been filmed in the late fifties. Soon Lily was immersed in the characters and the plot and loudly blew her nose to hold back tears at a tender scene. A light knock against the front door announced Jake's arrival. She opened the door, waved him inside and sniffled as he took the seat opposite her.

Jake eyed her curiously. "You sick?"

Lily sucked in a wobbly breath and pointed to the television screen with her index finger. "No...Gary Cooper's going to be killed in a couple of minutes and I hate to see him die."

Jake scooted forward in the thickly cushioned chair and linked his hands. "I talked to an old friend today."

Lily's eyes didn't leave the black-and-white picture tube. "That's nice."

"Rick's a downtown attorney and has made quite a name for himself in the past few years."

Lily didn't know why Jake found it so important to tell her about his friend in the middle of the best scene of the movie.

Jake hated it when Lily ignored him. He couldn't imagine how she could be so engrossed in a film that made her weep like a two-year-old. "Lily," he demanded, "would you listen to me?"

"In a minute," she sobbed, wrapping a handkerchief around her nose and blowing for all she was worth. Tears streamed down her cheeks and she wiped them aside with the back of her hand and sniffled anew.

Knowing that there wasn't anything he could do but wait, Jake settled back in the upholstered chair that had once belonged to a Zulu king and impatiently crossed his arms over his chest. He had terrific news for Lily—and she found it more important to cry over Gary Cooper than to listen to him. Women!

Ten minutes later, Lily stood and moved across the room to turn off the set. "Gee, that was a great movie."

"You cried through the whole thing," Jake admonished. He couldn't understand how she could cry as if the end of the world were upon them and think it was wonderful.

"I always cry during a Gary Cooper movie," she shot back. "I thought you knew that."

Rather than argue, Jake resumed his earlier position and leaned forward in the chair toward her. "As I was saying..."

"Do you want a cup of Marmite?" Remembering her manners, Lily felt guilty about being such a poor hostess. Gram had taught her better than this.

"What I want," Jake said with forced patience, "is for you to sit down and listen to me."

Meekly lowering herself to the sofa, Lily politely cupped her hands in her lap and looked toward Jake expectantly. "I'm ready."

"It's a damn good thing," he muttered.

"Well. I'm waiting." Sometimes it took Jake hours to get to the point. Not that he did a lot of talking. He'd say a few words here and there and she was expected to get the gist of his point. The problem was that Lily never did and he'd end up looking at her as if her head were full of holes.

"I saw Rick—my lawyer friend—this afternoon."

"The one from school?"

"Right. Anyway, Rick has become a regular social-ite in the past few years and he's invited me to a cock-tail party he's having Saturday night."

So! Lily blinked twice. She wouldn't have thought Jake would be so enthusiastic about a bunch of peo-ple standing around holding drinks and exchanging polite inanities. "That's interesting." She tried to hide a yawn and didn't succeed. Belatedly she cupped her mouth and expelled a long whiney breath.

Jake gave her one of his moody looks that curved up the edge of his mouth in a snarllike way. It was hap-pening already. Usually he didn't give her that look until he was five minutes into his monologue.

"I thought you'd be thrilled," he murmured, thinking how unappreciatively she was behaving, especially after everything he'd gone through. It hadn't been an easy thing to contact Rick—Mr. Success—and strike up a conversation after all those years.

"To be perfectly honest, I wouldn't have believed you'd enjoy a cocktail party."

"I won't. I'm doing it for you."

"For me?"

"There are bound to be a lot of rich men there, Lily. Undoubtedly some of them will be single and on the lookout for an attractive woman."

"What do you plan to do? Hand them my name and phone number?" she asked with pardonable exasperation.

"You're going with me," he barked, his own patience having reached its limit.

"Well, for heaven's sake, why didn't you say so?"

"Anyone with half a brain would have figured that out. You should know darn good and well that I wouldn't be willing do something as loony as attend a stupid party without a reason."

They stood facing each other, not more than two feet apart. The air between them was so heavy that Lily expected to see arcs of electricity spark and flash. Jake's breathing was heavy and rasping oddly. Hers wasn't any more even or controlled. They shouldn't be arguing—they were friends. Good friends.

Neither moved. Lily couldn't stop looking at him. They were so close that she could see every line in his handsome face, every groove, every pore. Even the hairs of his brows seemed overwhelmingly interesting. Her gaze located a faint scar on his jawline that she'd never noticed before and she wondered if this was a souvenir from Vietnam. He'd told her only a little of his experiences there.

His eyes were greener tonight than she'd remembered. Green as jade, dark as night, alive and glittering with an emotion Lily couldn't define. His mouth was relaxed and slightly parted as if beckoning her, telling her that she must make the first move. Surely she was reading him wrong. Jake wouldn't want to kiss her. They were friends—nothing more. What had happened in the attic had been a moment out of time and place. Still not believing what she saw, Lily raised her gaze to his and their eyes met and clashed. Jake did want to kiss her. And even more astonishing was that she wanted it, too. Jake must have seen the passion in her eyes, because his flared as if unwillingly drawn into something more powerful than his self-control.

"Lily." He breathed heavily and turned away from her, stalking to the opposite side of the room. "I think I will have something to drink after all."

"Marmite?" Somehow the one word made it through her parched lips.

"Sure—anything."

Lily was grateful that she had something to occupy her hands and her mind. Jake didn't follow her into the kitchen, and she needed to have time to compose her thoughts. Good grief, what was happening to them? After all these months there wasn't any logical explanation why they should suddenly be physically attracted to each other. Something must be in the air— but spring was nine months away. A laugh hovered on her lips as she pictured tiny neon lights that flashed on and off across her forehead, telling Jake: *Kiss Lily*. But Lily didn't want to kiss Jake; she was waiting for the right man. Jake was wonderful, but he wasn't the man for her, and they both knew it. Thank heaven Jake had exhibited enough sense to turn away when he did and thereby avoid a disaster. And that's exactly what it would have been.

Lily carried a steaming cup into the living room and carefully handed it to him. She wasn't as much afraid of being burned by the near-boiling water as she was fearful of her reaction if she touched him.

"I want you to attend that cocktail party with me." He picked up the conversation easily, pretending nothing had happened. Yet Jake knew they were both aware that they'd been a hair's breadth from hungrily falling into each other's arms.

"Saturday?" Her mind filled with niggling thoughts. She was scheduled to work, but she would be free at nine; she could wear her new dress. No, that was a bit too daring for a first meeting.

"Do you or don't you want to go?" Jake still hadn't taken a sip of his Marmite.

"Sure. I'll be happy to attend the party. Thanks for thinking of me." That sounded so stilted, Lily instantly wanted to grab back the words and tell him how pleased she was that he'd thought of her and was willing to help her secure her goal.

"I'll see you Saturday, then."

"Saturday," she echoed, and watched as Jake set aside his untouched drink and walked out of the house.

Lily didn't see Jake for two days. That wasn't as unusual as it was unsettling. It was almost as if they were afraid to see each other again.

During that time, Lily thought about Jake. She didn't know what was happening, but it had to stop. Jake was the antithesis of everything she wanted in a man. He had no real ambitions and was perfectly content to live his days lackadaisically aboard his sailboat and do nothing more than write short stories that didn't pay. Usually he received three free copies of the publication in compensation for his hundred hours of sweat and toil. Sometimes Lily wondered why Jake wrote—each word seemed so painful for him. Jake was a paradoxical sort of person. He hid behind the keys of his typewriter and revealed his soul in heart-wrenching stories no one would ever read.

While Jake was perfectly content with his life, Lily desperately wanted to improve hers. She longed to explore the world, to travel the Orient Express and dine in the shadow of the Eiffel Tower. She yearned to see China and lazily soak up the sun on a South Pacific island. And when she went shopping, Lily didn't want to ever look at a price tag again. Bargain basements and secondhand stores would all be part of a past she longed to bury. But most of all, Lily never wanted to hear "Moon River" again.

On Saturday evening Lily dressed carefully in her gold lamé gown. Her dark curls were swirled high on her head and held in place with combs her father had brought her from India when she was twelve. He'd died shortly afterward and Lily had treasured this last gift, wearing them only on the most special occasions. She spent an hour in front of the mirror practicing a sultry smile, and decided against the voluptuous approach. Instead of looking sensual and alluring, Lily decided she resembled someone who was coming down with a liver ailment.

At the end of her shift, with the thirty-ninth version of "Moon River" ringing in her ears, Lily stepped out of the hotel, expecting Jake to meet her. She didn't see him, and for half a second panic filled her.

"Lily," Jake said, stepping forward.

Lily blinked and placed her hand over her heart at the sight of the tall, handsome man who stood directly in front of her. "Jake, is that you?"

"Who else were you expecting? Prince Charming?"

"You're wearing a suit!" A gray one that could have been lifted directly from the pages of *Gentlemen's Quarterly*, Lily realized in bemusement. The simple, understated pattern of the fabric in the neutral color was perfect for Jake, emphasizing his broad shoulders and muscular build. "You look wonderful!"

Jake ran his finger along the inside of his collar as if he needed the extra room to breathe properly. "I don't feel that way."

"But why?" She'd never seen Jake in anything dressier than slacks and a fisherman's bulky-knit sweater.

"Hell, I don't know. Knowing Rick, I figure this party is going to be an elaborate affair and it's best to dress the part."

Lily could hardly take her eyes from him. Jake made a dashing figure. Her gaze dropped to her own much-worn dress. "How do I look? Am I over-dressed? Should I wear a lighter perfume? I don't want to give anyone the wrong impression." Her own insecurities dulled the naturally dark brilliance of her eyes.

Jake glanced at her and shrugged his shoulders. "You look all right."

All right! She'd spent half the day getting ready, fussing over each minute detail until nothing looked right anymore. "I hope you know that you're about as romantic as the underside of a toad."

"Listen, Bright Eyes, if you want romance, try Paul Newman. I ain't your man."

"You're telling me!" she huffed.

"Listen, are we going to this fiasco or not?" He held the taxi passenger door open for her, but didn't wait until she was inside before walking around the front of the car.

The first ten minutes of the ride down Golden Gate Avenue past the Civic Center was spent in complete silence.

Lily felt obligated to wade into the uneasy stillness first. Both of them were fidgety and on edge. "I didn't know you owned a suit."

Jake's response was little short of a grunt. The expensive suit had been Elaine's idea. She was the one who'd insisted he needed some decent clothes. She had dragged him around town to several exclusive men's stores and fussed over him like a drone over a queen bee. He'd detested every second of it, but he'd been so crazy about her that he'd stood there like a stooge and done exactly as she dictated. His weak-mindedness shocked him now. In thinking over his short but fiery relationship with Elaine, Jake was dismayed by some of the things he'd allowed her to do to him. The last party he'd attended had been with Elaine. He'd sat back and listened as she introduced him to her rich friends, telling them that Jake owned his own company and lived on a yacht. To hear her tell it, Jake was a business tycoon. In reality, he owned one taxicab that he drove himself, and his "yacht" was a ten-year-old, twenty-seven-foot, single-mast, fore- and aft-rigged sailboat that most of Elaine's colleagues could have bought with their pocket change.

"Are you going to sit there and sulk all night?" Lily questioned, growing impatient.

"Men never sulk," Jake declared, feeling smug about defending his fellow man.

"Are you suggesting that women do?" Lily was starting to feel irritated.

"If the shoe fits..." Jake was beginning to get cocky. Never again would he allow a woman to dictate to him. He was as free as a flounder and he planned to stay that way.

"Well, hello there, Betsy," she said in a singsong, sarcastic voice.

"Betsy?" His eyes momentarily left the road to flash her a puzzled look. "What do you mean?"

"Well, I'd say that you're acting suspiciously like a female, sitting there sulking."

Jake struggled to compose an appropriately witty response that would put Lily in her place, when Rick's house came into view. He parked several yards away in the closest available space. His five-year-old Chevy looked incongruous on the same street with all the fancy foreign cars, so he patted his steering wheel affectionately as if to assure his taxi that it was as good as the rest of them.

Rick's house was ostentatious colonial-style, with thick white pillars and a well-lit front entrance. Jake swallowed nervously. Ole Rick had done well for himself, even better than Jake had assumed.

"It's lovely," Lily murmured, and sighed with humble appreciation. This was exactly the kind of home she longed to own someday—one with crystal chandeliers, Persian carpets and gold fixtures.

"Lovely if you like that sort of thing," Jake grumbled under his breath.

Lily liked it just fine. "Oh, but I do. Thank you, Jake."

The genuine emotion in her voice was a surprise and he tore his gaze away from the house long enough to glance her way.

"I should have been more appreciative. I'd never thought I'd be able attend something as wonderful as this. Oh, Jake, just think of all the wealthy men who'll be here."

"I'm thinking," he mumbled, pleased for the first time that he'd accepted Rick's invitation.

If Lily was impressed with the outside of Jake's friend's house, she was doubly so with the interior. She resisted the urge to run her hand over the polished mahogany woodwork and refused to stare at the Oriental rugs. A maid perfunctorily accepted their coats at the front door and directed them toward a central room where drinks were being served.

"Jake, ole buddy."

Lily sensed Jake stiffen, but was proud of the way he disguised his uneasiness and shook hands with the short man with a receding hairline. Lily could picture the man as a successful attorney. She could see him pacing in front of the jury box and glancing acrimoniously toward the defendant.

"Rick," Jake said with a rare smile. "It's good to see you. Thanks for the invitation."

"Any time." Although he spoke to Jake, Rick's gaze rested on Lily. "Jake, introduce me to this sweet cream puff."

"Rick, Lily. Lily, Rick."

"I'm most pleased to make your acquaintance," Lily murmured demurely. "Jake has told me so much about you."

Briefly, Rick's enthralled gaze left Lily to glance at Jake. "Where did you find this jewel?"

Lily's gaze pleaded with Jake not to tell Rick the real story of Gram confronting the Wheaton manager in full witch doctor's costume, outraged over Lily's starting wages. Jake had come to Gram's rescue and as a reward, Gram had chanted a few words over Jake and told him that his life would be richly blessed.

"We met at the Wheaton," Jake explained and Lily reached for his hand, squeezing it as a means of thanking him.

"Are you visiting our fair city?" Rick directed the question to her.

"No, I play the piano there."

"A musician!" Rick exclaimed. "I imagine you're a woman of many talents."

Jake didn't know what Rick was implying, but he didn't like the sound of it. He bunched up his fist until he realized that Lily's fingers were linked with his and he forced his hand to relax.

"Only a few talents, I fear," Lily answered with such aplomb that Jake wanted to kiss her. "But enough to impress my friends."

"Then I'd consider it an honor to be your friend."

Lily batted her long lashes at the successful attorney. "Perhaps."

From the way Rick's eyes widened, Jake knew that Lily had impressed his former associate. A surge of pride filled Jake and he struggled not to put his arm over Lily's soft shoulders.

Rick claimed Lily's hand. "Do you mind if I steal your girl away for a few minutes?"

Jake did mind, but this was exactly why he'd brought Lily to the party. She would make more contacts here than during a year of playing piano at the Wheaton. "Feel free," he murmured, lifting a glass of champagne from the tray of the passing server. He didn't watch as Lily and Rick crossed the room, Lily's arm tucked securely in the crook of Rick's elbow.

The bubbling liquid in the narrow crystal glass seemed to be laughing at him and, almost angrily, Jake set it aside. He hated champagne and always had. He much preferred a hearty burgundy with some soul to it. His tastes were robust, and he repeatedly had to remind himself that Lily was meant to drink champagne, not moderately priced wine.

He found an obscure corner and sat down, giving anyone who approached him a look that would discourage even the most stouthearted. He could hear Lily's musical laugh drift from another section of the house and was pleased she was enjoying the party. At least one of them was having a decent time.

Another waiter came past and Jake ordered ouzo, a Greek drink. Gram had given him his first taste of the anise-flavored liqueur she drank regularly. Lily claimed it had made her teeth go soft, and to be honest, the licorice-tasting drink had curled a few of Jake's chest hairs. But he was in the mood for it tonight—something potent to remind himself that he was doing the noble thing. Now he knew how Joan of Arc must have felt as she was tied to the stake and the torches were aimed at the dry straw. No, he was being melodramatic again. What did it matter? He'd known all along that he was going to lose *his* Lily. The thought crystalized in his brain: Lily wasn't his; had never been his. He drank down the liqueur with one swallow and felt it sear a path to his stomach. Lily was his friend, his good friend. He'd do anything for her and Gram—well, almost anything.

Jake asked for another ouzo and drank it down with the same alacrity as the first. Another followed shortly after that. His eyes found a woman sitting on the sofa on the other side of the room, and she smiled. Hey, Jake mused, maybe this party wasn't such a loss after all. Maybe Lily wasn't the only one destined to have a good time.

He stood, surprised that a house as expensive as Rick's had a floor that swayed like a ship at sea. Suavely, he tucked one hand in his pants pocket and paused to smooth the hair along the side of his head. There wasn't any need to look like a slob.

Just when he was prepared to introduce himself to Goldilocks across the way, he heard the piano and stopped cold. "Moon River." Oh no. Rick had convinced Lily to entertain him. Jake knew how she felt about that song. Rick couldn't do that to Lily. Jake wouldn't let him. Rushing forward, he raised his hand and started to say something when the floor suddenly, unexpectedly, came rushing up to meet him.

"Jake." The soft, soothing voice sounded like an angel's and Jake struggled to open his eyes. The piercing overhead light hurt and he lifted his hand to protect his eyes from the glare. He was astonished to feel heavy bandages wrapped across his forehead. His head felt as if little men were standing at his temples and alternately pounding away with miniature sledge-hammers.

"What happened?" His words were barely audible. He swallowed and moistened his mouth, which felt like the bottom of San Francisco Bay.

"You're going to be fine."

Jake recognized the voice as Lily's. "The hell I am." The volume of his own voice caused him to wince. "What happened?" he repeated, much quieter this time. "Where am I?"

"You fell, and to be on the safe side, Rick insisted that we call an ambulance."

Jake snorted. Sure, Rick would say that. He'd fallen in Rick's house and Rick wanted to be damn sure Jake would have no cause to sue him.

"I'm at the hospital?"

"They've given you ten stitches. It was a nasty cut."

Rolling his head to the side, Jake avoided the light glaring down at him from a thousand-watt bulb. Something was wrong, and his eyes refused to focus properly. Instead of the lovely gold dress Lily had worn to the party she was dressed in red. He tried to swing his legs off the table and properly investigate his circumstances.

"Jake," Lily cried, her sweet angel's voice laced with concern. "Lie still."

"I want out of here."

"Oh, Jake, no. Rick has insisted the hospital keep you overnight for observation."

"Like hell."

"Would you stop swearing?" she admonished. "Now don't worry about anything. Rick's picking up the tab."

Swear! If she knew the thoughts that were going through his head she'd blush from now until doomsday. "Lily, I want out of here. And for heaven's sake, what happened to your dress? It's covered with blood.''

Lily didn't ever want to feel again the terror that gripped her the moment she'd seen Jake lying on the floor. She'd rushed to him and lifted his bleeding head into her lap. "Honestly, you scared me half out of my wits. Now don't argue. I'll be back in the morning. Just take care of yourself and don't worry about a thing.''

"Lily." His hand held her fast to his side. "How will you get home?''

"Don't worry. Rick's taking me. And before you feel guilty over my dress, Rick wants to buy me another one to replace it." She leaned over him and lightly brushed her lips over his. "Good night, Jake. Sleep well and take care of yourself. I insist.''

The sound of her clicking shoes told him she was leaving. The feeling came again—the sensation that told him something was awry—and for the second time it had to do with Lily. Rick wasn't right for her, either, and Jake had to find some way to put an end to that relationship before it got started.

Chapter Four

Holding a small bouquet of flowers, Lily traipsed through the hospital lobby to the open elevator, stepped inside and pushed the button for the appropriate floor. She'd been worried about Jake all night. He'd looked so pale against the starched white hospital sheets. Pale and confused. Lily should never have left his side, but Rick had convinced her that there wasn't any more either of them could do. Jake had been given a shot and would soon be asleep. Nonetheless, Lily had lingered outside the hall until the shot took effect, then reluctantly left.

When the heavy metal doors of the elevator parted, Lily stepped out eagerly. She had so much to tell Jake. He'd been such a dear to have taken her to the party. Everything had turned out beautifully—except for his fall, of course. Lily had met several men, all of whom had an aura of wealth. She prided herself on her ability to recognize money when she saw it. Rick had insisted on buying her a new dress since her gold lamé was so badly stained. But Lily had adamantly refused. The evening gown wasn't ruined. Gram had used vinegar and a few other inventively chosen ingredients to remove Jake's blood from her dress.

Lily stepped past the nurse's station and headed down the wide hall to Jake's room. The faint smell of antiseptic caused her to wrinkle her nose. Jake would be glad to get out of there.

The door to his room was open and Lily paused in the doorway, looking at the nurse's aide who was stripping the bed of the sheets and blankets. Troubled, Lily's gaze slid to the number printed on the door for a second time to be sure she had the right room.

"Good morning," Lily murmured.

"Morning," the other woman answered flatly. "Is there something I can do for you?"

"Do you know where Jake Carson is?"

"Mr. Carson released himself early this morning."

Lily swallowed to relieve her voice of its shock and surprise. "Released himself? But why?"

"I believe Mr. Carson had several reasons, all of which were described in colorful detail."

"Oh, dear." Lily was shocked to realize she'd spoken out loud.

"I'm afraid so. He also insisted on paying his own tab and wanted the bill brought to him immediately." Impatiently, the woman jerked the bottom sheet from the raised hospital bed. "I've seen a few stubborn men in my day, but that one takes the cake."

It didn't take much imagination for Lily to picture the scene. Jake could be a terror when he wanted to be, and from the frustrated look on the nurse's flushed face, Jake had outdone himself this time. Lily was all the more convinced that she shouldn't have left him. She shouldn't have listened to Rick. Next time, she'd follow her instincts.

"Did he say where he was going?" Lily pressed.

The woman hugged the sheet to her abdomen and slowly shook her head. "No, but I'm sure the staff could give you a few suggestions about where we'd like to see him."

"I am sorry." Lily felt obliged to apologize for Jake, although she was convinced he wouldn't appreciate it. "I'm sure he didn't mean . . . whatever it was he said."

"He meant it," the woman growled, placing the sheet with unnecessary force inside a laundry cart at her side.

"Well, thank you, anyway," Lily stammered. "And here . . ." She shoved the small bouquet of daisies into the woman's hands. "Please take these." With that, Lily turned and hurried from the room.

By the time she arrived back at Gram's, Lily was worried and confused. "Gram, Jake's left the hospital."

Gram stood at the ironing board, pressing dried flowers between sheets of waxed paper. "I know."

"You know!"

"Why yes. He phoned earlier."

"Where is he?" Lily demanded, the wobble in her voice betraying her concern. "The hospital said he released himself."

"That's what he said," Gram said, and moved from the iron to the stove where she stirred a mysterious green concoction. Lily knew better than to inquire into

Gram's cooking. Taste was what mattered. Sometimes it was best not to know the ingredients.

"He shouldn't be alone... not with a head injury."

"He sounded perfectly fine," Gram contradicted.

"Is he at the marina? I should probably go there, don't you think? He shouldn't be alone at a time like this. Something could happen." Not waiting for a response, Lily made a sharp about-face and headed out of the kitchen. For a panicked second, Lily imagined a dizzy, disoriented Jake stumbling about the sailboat. He could slip and fall overboard and no one would ever know.

"It'd be a waste of time."

"A waste of time? Why? Lily paused and turned around to face Gram, her thoughts scrambled.

Humming an old Glenn Miller tune, Gram continued stirring. "Jake's on his way over here."

"Now?"

"That's what he said."

"Why didn't you tell me that earlier?" Lily cried.

For the first time, Gram turned away from the stove and studied Lily with narrowed, knowing eyes. "You seem worried, girl. Jake can take care of himself."

"I know... but he's lost a lot of blood. He had ten stitches and..."

"He's not going to appreciate it if you make a fuss over him."

Lily forced the tense muscles of her back and shoulders to relax. Gram was right. Jake would hate it if he had even a inkling of how concerned she was.

"What else did he say?" Trying to disguise how disquieting Lily found this entire matter, she pushed the kitchen chair under the table.

"Do you want some split-pea soup?" Gram answered Lily's question with one of her own, infuriating Lily. There was no rushing Gram, who seemed to take life in lazy strides, loping along without a care.

"No, thanks." An involuntary grimace crossed her face. Gram loved split-pea soup, but Lily didn't know why she would be eating it now. It was only midmorning.

A loud knock against the front door announced Jake's arrival. Lily battled the urge to run across the room to meet him.

Without waiting for someone to open the door, Jake let himself inside. "Morning."

"Hello, Jake." Demurely, Lily laced her fingers in front of her. "How are you feeling?"

"Great," he answered shortly, walking past her into the kitchen.

"Soup's ready," Lily heard her grandmother tell him.

"I appreciate it, Gram."

"When it comes to restoring a person's health, it's better than chicken noodle."

"Anything you cook is better than my futile attempts."

Shocked and a little hurt at Jake's abrupt greeting, Lily stood stiffly, halfway between the kitchen and the front door. Jake may have said only one word to her, but his eyes had spelled out volumes. The most amazing thing about Jake was his eyes. Often over the past year they had informed her of what he was thinking and feeling before he could say a word. They were a stormy shade of jade when he was angry, and that seemed to be happening on a regular basis lately. At other times they were a murky green, but that was generally when he was troubled about something. Then there were rare times when they sparked with what seemed a thousand tiny lights when he was surprised or fascinated with something. They'd glittered like that recently, when he'd first seen her in the dress she'd bought with Gram's bingo winnings and again later, when they'd met before Rick's party. However, his eyes had quickly changed to that murky shade of green. Lily didn't know what to make of Jake anymore. He'd been so easy to read and understand in the past, but either he was changing or she was losing her ability to understand the one man she thought she knew so well.

"How are you feeling?" Lily asked for the second time, coming into the kitchen.

Jake had pulled out the chair she'd recently pushed under the table, and sat drinking Gram's soup from a ceramic mug.

"Fine," he answered without looking at her.

"You look better." Some color had returned to his face. Yet he remained so pale that the tiny crease lines etched about his eyes and mouth were more noticeable than ever.

Gram joined Jake at the table, pouring equal portions of the soup into two additional mugs. "Here." She gave one to Lily who looked down on it and wrinkled up her nose.

"No thanks, I prefer chicken noodle."

Jake's snort was almost imperceptible. "I'll be ready in a minute here," he added.

Lily glanced at Gram, who appeared oblivious to the comment. "Ready for what?" Lily inquired.

"Shopping."

"You're going shopping?" Good grief, he'd just been released from the hospital. "Whatever for?" If he needed anything, she'd be happy to make the trip for him.

"We're going out."

"Us?"

Jake caught Gram's eye. "You didn't tell her?"

"I didn't get a chance."

"Tell me what?" Lily demanded, not liking the way Jake spoke to Gram and ignored her.

"Jake's taking you out to buy you a new dress." Gram informed her.

"The dress is fine," Lily protested loudly. "Didn't you tell him that?"

"I did," Gram huffed. "But he insists."

Jake's gaze bounced from Gram to Lily and back again. "Did you tell Lily that it won't do any good to argue with me on this one? I saw what I did to her dress. I'm buying her another one and that's all there is to it."

Lily sank into the chair across from Jake and boldly met his gaze. "In case you hadn't noticed, I'm standing right here. There's no need to ask Gram to tell me anything when you and I are separated by less than two feet." The words came out sharp and argumentative despite her effort to sound casual and offhanded.

"If you insist." He quirked a dark brow in arrogant speculation, but dry laughter coated his voice.

Gram apparently noticed it too, and chuckled delightedly. "You two youngsters remind me of Paddy and me."

Paddy was Lily's grandfather. He'd died several years before Lily was born, and the tales Gram had told of her beloved were an indication of the deep love and commitment her grandparents had shared. Lily hoped to share the same deep and lasting love with her own husband.

"You ready?" Jake asked, standing.

Lily looked at Gram for support, then back to Jake. "I hate to have you spend money on me. It isn't necessary."

"Would you like it better if Rick bought you a dress? Is that it?"

"Of course not." She hardly knew Rick and didn't want him buying her clothes.

"Then let's get this over and done with." He was halfway across the living room before Lily moved.

"Gram, what's wrong with Jake? He's not himself."

Gram shook her pin-curled head and laughed. "I can't say I rightly know, but I have my suspicions. I'm not so old not to have my suspicions."

With Gram speaking in riddles and Jake marching ahead, Lily had little choice but to follow him. He was sitting in the driver's seat of his taxi and glaring impatiently toward Lily as she came down the front steps.

"How'd you get your cab back?" she asked, opening the car door. They'd left it parked in front of Rick's house and Lily had wondered if Jake wanted her and Gram to pick it up for him. That was one of the things she'd planned to ask him that morning at the hospital.

"I have my ways," he grumbled, checking the side-view mirror before pulling onto the street. A heavy pause followed. "Did you have a good time last night?"

The question repeated in Lily's mind. Had she? Yes and no. The evening had been one she'd dreamed about for years. She'd met several interesting men who would suit her purpose nicely. Rick had been a gentleman, kind and considerate and genuinely concerned when Jake had fallen. He'd taken charge immediately and known what to do, acting quickly. For her own part, Lily was shocked at her response to Jake's injury. She'd fallen to pieces, and Rick had been there to lend his support. She could never thank him enough.

"Well?" Jake asked again. "Did you or did you not have a good time?"

"The evening was grand. Thank you, Jake, for making everything so special."

"Did you meet someone?" Anticipating her answer, his grip tightened around the hard steering wheel. He wanted Lily to assure him that she had found the rich man of her dreams. But in the same breath, he wanted her to tell him she'd found no one.

"Not really."

"What about Rick?"

"He was very nice."

The corner of Jake's mouth curved up sarcastically. What a weak word *nice* was. No woman would ever describe him that way. The thought was comforting. "Anyone else?"

"Not really. A couple of others said they planned to visit the Wheaton to hear me play, but I don't think they'll show."

"Who?" Jake demanded.

Lily lifted one shoulder in a delicate shrug, surprised that Jake would sound angry when meeting eligible wealthy men was the reason he'd taken her to the party. "I don't remember their names."

"If they do come, I want to know about it so I can have them checked out." He was eager to know for other reasons as well—ones that weren't clearly defined in his mind. He wanted Lily married and happy and he wished to God that he could forget the taste of her mouth. Every time he looked at her, he had trouble not sampling the sweetness of her kiss. He'd received a head injury, Jake told himself. One that was apparently affecting his reasoning ability. He shouldn't be thinking of Lily in that way. His only option was to marry her off to Rick or one of the others—and quickly.

"Jake," Lily said his name with a softness that stirred his insides.

"Yes?" Involuntarily, his hands tightened around the steering wheel.

"Why are you insisting on buying me a dress?"

"What's the matter? Do you think Rick could afford a better one?"

"Oh, Jake, of course not."

From the soft catch in her voice, Jake knew he'd hurt her to even imply such a thing. "It's a matter of pride," he explained after a lengthy pause. "You told me Rick wanted to replace the one I ruined. My blood stained it, so I should be the one to buy you another dress."

"But Gram got the stain out."

"It doesn't matter."

"But..."

"I'm buying you the damn dress. Understand?"

She didn't answer.

"Understand?" he repeated forcefully.

"Repeaters is off Thirty-second."

"What?"

"The secondhand store where I usually buy my dresses." It took a supreme act of will to give in to his pride. Jake had always been so reasonable, but the harsh tone of his voice told Lily she'd best concede gracefully. Either Jake would go with her or he'd buy something for her on his own.

"I'm not getting you anything secondhand."

"All right," she agreed reluctantly. "Either Sears or Penney's is fine."

"We're going to Neiman-Marcus."

"Neiman-Marcus, Jake!" Lily's jaw sagged open. Jake couldn't afford to shop there.

The announcement came out as much of a shock to Jake as it apparently did to Lily. He hadn't given the matter much thought and had driven toward the downtown area, thinking he'd decide where they'd shop once he'd found parking. But after he spoke the words he decided, *Well, why not!* If he was going to buy Lily a dress it would be one she'd remember all her life.

"I saw a dress I liked on display in Penney's." Lily attempted the tactful approach. Her hands felt clammy just at the thought of spending all Jake's money on some silly gown. He worked too hard and saved so little.

"And I saw one at Neiman-Marcus," Jake countered. "You're always talking about how you want to shop there someday. I'm giving you the chance."

A hundred arguments crossed her mind as they located parking and Jake escorted her through the plush interior of the elite department store.

"Jake," Lily pleaded anew.

"And nothing on sale." Jake paused in front of a mannequin. "Nice," he said to no one in particular.

"It should be," Lily informed him stiffly, reading the price tag. "This little piece of chiffon is five hundred dollars."

It demanded all of his discipline for Jake to reveal none of his thoughts. Five hundred dollars for a dress! He had no idea. He had wanted to buy Lily a dress, not invest in the future. He hesitated a fraction of a second longer. "So?"

"Jake, honestly, five hundred dollars would wipe you out." Lily was growing more uneasy by the minute. This whole idea was ridiculous. Pride or not, Jake had no business buying her clothes. Not here.

"May I help you?" An attentive salesclerk approached them.

"Yes," Jake insisted.

"No," Lily countered.

"Perhaps if I came back in a few minutes." The salesclerk took a step in retreat.

"My friend here would like to try on this dress," Jake said, lifting the hem of the peach-colored chiffon on the mannequin.

"Jake," Lily hissed under her breath.

"And a few more just like this," Jake continued.

The clerk gave a polite nod. "If you'll come this way."

Jake's hand on the small of Lily's back urged her forward.

"Do you have any color in mind?"

"Midnight blue, red, and maybe something white." The choices came off the top of his head. Once, a long time back, it had occurred to him that with Lily's dark hair she'd look like an angel in white.

"I have just the thing." The clerk motioned toward the dressing rooms on the other side of the spacious floor.

Like a small duckling marching after its mother, Lily walked behind the salesclerk through rows and rows of expensive, elaborate dresses.

Sitting in a deep, cushioned chair outside the dressing room, Jake leaned against the padded back and crossed his legs, playing the part of a generous benefactor. Absently, he wished he had a cigar to smoke. This was just the type of thing Rick would relish. Jake had recognized the look in Rick's eyes the minute Lily had been introduced. Rick had wanted her. Jake could understand the feeling. He'd wanted Elaine from the first minute he'd seen her; had lusted after her and been so thoroughly infatuated with her that he'd been completely duped. But Lily was different. She wasn't Elaine—knowledgeable in the ways of the world, practiced in the means of obtaining her own way with men. No, Lily was an innocent.

Changing positions, Jake uncrossed his legs and folded his arms over his chest. He didn't know what could be taking so long. Depending on the dress Lily chose, he had to come up with a way of paying for it. Salvaging his pride was worth five hundred of his hard-earned dollars if that was what it took. He hoped, however, that it wouldn't.

"Jake," Lily whispered, coming out of the dressing room. She wore a deep-blue dress with a scalloped collar and short sleeves. "How do you like it?"

Jake watched her walk self-consciously in front of him. It was a dress, nothing special. "What do you think?" he asked.

"The saleslady called it Spun Sapphires."

"It has a name?"

"Yes." She inserted her hand inside the thin belt. "It's a little big around the waist."

"Then try on another."

Relieved, Lily returned to the dressing room. Spun Sapphires was nice, but she hated the thought of Jake spending four hundred dollars on a single dress. As tactfully as possible she asked the clerk to bring in dresses that weren't in the same price category. Willing to please, the woman had returned with a variety in the colors Jake had requested. A white frock of crepe with feminine tucks and simulated pearl buttons down the front caught her eye.

Jake felt conspicuous and ill-at-ease. Since 'Nam he liked to think of himself as an island, an entity unto himself. His life was comfortable. He needed no one. There were no ties to the mainland, no bridges, no sandbars. Nothing. Elaine had been the first to tug him closer to the shore. And now Lily... Just when he wanted to cast thoughts of her from his mind, he glanced up to discover her standing in front of him. She wore a simple, white dress and was so breathtakingly beautiful that he felt the air constrict in his lungs. Without realizing what he was doing, he slowly rose to his feet. Their eyes met and held an instant before Lily's thick lashes fanned downward. Jake could hardly breathe, let alone comment. He'd never seen anyone more beautiful.

"What's the name of this one?" he asked, shocked at how weak his voice sounded. He swallowed and held his breath, trying not to notice that Lily was a vision of loveliness in the white dress. The task was impossible. She was more than winsome; she was everything pure and good that Jake had ever sought in a woman. With all that was in him, he longed to smooth her perfectly arched brows. His fingers ached with the need to trace her cheekbones and touch the fullness of her provocative mouth.

"It's called Angel's Breath." Her voice sounded as unsteady as his own.

"We'll take it," Jake informed the salesclerk, but he didn't look toward her. Tearing his eyes from Lily would have been unthinkable. Like a man seeing an apparition, he wanted to hold the memory of her in his mind and carry it with him for the remainder of his days.

"But you don't even know how much it is," Lily objected.

"The price doesn't matter." Her nose was perfect, Jake decided, with a soft sprinkling of freckles across the narrow bridge. He adored every single one of them.

Jake paid the salesclerk while Lily changed clothes. The woman smiled warmly at him as he presented her with the check for a hundred and sixty-five dollars. On Lily that dress would have been a bargain at twice the price.

"The dress is lovely on your wife," she told him with a sincerity Jake couldn't doubt. It wasn't until they were at the car that Jake realized he hadn't corrected the salesclerk. Lily wasn't his wife and he was doing everything he could to marry her off to a wealthy man so she could have the things in life she longed for most. When the time came, he'd let her go without a regret. When the time came...but not today.

"Thank you, Jake," Lily told him once they were outside the store.

He looked down at her, captivated by the warmth of her smile. "Any time." He reached for her hand, linking their fingers. "Are you hungry?"

"Starved. But it's my turn to treat you. What would you like?"

"Food."

"That's what I love most about you," Lily teased. "You're so articulate." The word *love* echoed in the corners of her mind, sending a shaft of sensation racing through her to land in the pit of her stomach. She did love Jake, but not the way her mind was indicating. He was her friend, her co-conspirator, a family friend. Nothing less—and everything more.

They took the cable car down to Fisherman's Wharf and stood in line with hordes of tourists. Lily's favorite part of San Francisco was the waterfront. The air smelled of saltwater and deep-fried fish. The breeze off the bay was cool and refreshing and Lily could have spent the entire day doing nothing more than drifting from one small shop to another, buying nothing but admiring all that she saw. They ate their lunch on the sandy beach behind the Maritime Museum. Lily took off her sandals and stepped to the water's edge, teasing the tide and running back to Jake when the chilly water touched her toes. For his part, Jake leaned against the mattress of sand and closed his eyes. Lily's musical laugh lulled him into a light slumber. He was content with his world, content to have Lily at his side, satisfied with life. He thought about the characters in the short story he'd mailed off recently to the *New Yorker*. Lily had claimed it was his best story and had encouraged him to aim for the top with this one. Personally, Jake thought it was a waste of time but to appease her, he'd sent it to the New York publisher.

"Jake?"

"Hmm?" Lily sat at his side, drawing up her legs so that her arms crossed her knees.

"It's almost four."

"Already?" He sat up. The day had slipped past so quickly that he couldn't remember its passing.

"You're not working tonight, are you?"

"No." Lily hesitated. Jake knew her schedule as well as she did.

"Good." He settled back on the sand, folding his arms behind his head. "I'm too relaxed to move."

"Me, too," Lily said with a sigh and joined him, lying back in the sand. They were so close that their thighs touched and Jake squeezed his eyes shut at the surge of emotion that burned through him at the merest brush of her leg against his. Slow, silent seconds ticked past, but Lily didn't move and Jake hadn't the will. The summer air felt heavy with unspoken thoughts and labored heartbeats. It demanded everything within Jake not to reach for Lily's hand and crush her fingers with his own. He felt close to her, closer than he had any right. His heart groaned. Lily wasn't Lily to him anymore, but a beautiful, enticing, slender and soft woman. He couldn't ignore her any longer. Dear God, what had gotten into him?

"Jake?"

He rolled his head to the side and their eyes met, brilliant green clashing with magnificent brown. Her warm breath fanned his face. "Yes?"

"I've enjoyed today."

"Me, too."

"Can we do it again?"

Jake turned his head and stared into the clear blue sky. For a long minute he didn't say anything. He couldn't do this again soon and remain sane; having Lily this close and not touching her was the purest form of torture. He could never be the man she wanted. "I don't know." He would probably do them both a favor if he got out of her life and settled down the coast someplace. That was the nice thing about owning a sailboat and driving a taxi; he could move on without a string of responsibilities tying him down.

"You're right," Lily concurred. "It's probably not a good idea."

"Why?" Something perverse within him insisted that he ask.

"Well..." Lily hedged, uncertain. "Just because."

"Right," he agreed. "Just because." Standing up, Jake wiped the granules of sand from his clothes. "I think I should take you home."

"You probably should." But Lily's tone lacked enthusiasm. The day had been charmed, a gift she had never expected to receive. "Gram will wonder about us."

"We might cool her wrath if we bring a peace offering," Jake suggested, wanting to put a semblance of balance back into their day. They should have been laughing and joking instead of walking around with sad faces. The day with Lily was special and one he would long remember.

"How do you propose doing that?"

"Chinese food."

"But Jake..."

"Gram loves it."

"I know, but—"

"No buts."

Lily tried to talk to him twice on the way through Chinatown. Jake knew his way around, popping in and out of stores, greeting friends and exchanging pleasantries along the way. As much as possible, Jake ignored Lily.

"I didn't know you spoke Chinese," Lily commented, hurrying after him.

"Only a little." He didn't mention that half of everything he'd said had been an explanation about Lily.

"Not from what I heard."

"I'm a man of many talents," he joked, loading her arms with the brown paper sacks that contained their meal.

Again on the way home, Lily tried to talk to Jake, but he sang at the top of his lungs, infecting her with his good mood. Soon Lily's sweet voice joined his own. At a stoplight, their smiling eyes met briefly and the song died on his lips. Without thinking, Jake leaned over and touched his lips to hers. His hand brushed the hair from her temple and lingered in the thick dark strands.

A blaring horn behind him rudely reminded Jake that the light had changed. Forcing himself to sing again, Jake stepped on the accelerator and sped ahead.

Lily had a more difficult time recovering from the casual kiss. It felt so extraordinarily right to have Jake claim her lips as if he'd been doing it for a lifetime. His light touch left her longing for more.

When Jake glanced at her curiously out of the corner of his eye, she forced her voice to join his, but it wasn't the same and both of them knew it.

Jake eased to a stop in front of the house. Gram was standing on the front porch, her hands riding her round hips as she paced the small area. "It's about time you got home, girl. Rick called. He's on his way over."

Chapter Five

The sensation of dread went all the way through Jake. He hadn't been entirely obtuse. He'd known from the minute they entered Chinatown that Lily had been trying to talk to him. But in his stupidity, Jake feared that she was going to mention things he didn't want to discuss—mainly that something rare and special was happening between them. Such talk was best delayed and, if possible, ignored entirely.

"Rick's coming?" he questioned, turning to Lily, doing his damnedest to disguise the raging battle that was going on inside him. Rick was better for Lily than he'd ever be. Rick could give her the things she craved. But Jake didn't like it. Not one bit. There was something very wrong about spending the day with Lily and then watching her march off with Rick that evening. His gut instinct told him Rick was wrong for Lily, but he couldn't say anything without making a fool of himself. He'd been doing enough of that lately as it was.

"I tried to tell you earlier," she mumbled, feeling guilty and wretched. "I...we...Rick and I, that is, we're going to dinner..."

"No problem," he said, feigning a shrug of indifference. "Gram and I will have a good time without you." He walked ahead of Lily and took the older woman by the waist. "I guess you're stuck with me tonight."

"I'd consider it a privilege," Gram told him with a rare, toothy smile.

Jake responded with one of his own. He led the way into the house, carrying the sacks of spicy Chinese food to the kitchen. If Lily wore the white dress he bought her, he'd have one hell of a time accepting it. She couldn't. Not after what they'd shared today. Somehow, deep inside him, Jake knew she wouldn't do that to him.

Lily walked to her room with all the enthusiasm of someone going to the dentist for a root canal. She felt terrible. Everything had been so perfect today with Jake. When they'd stopped at the red light and Jake had kissed her, Lily had died a little. The kiss had felt so good. So right—as natural as though Jake had been kissing her for years and they were meant to be together forever. Only they weren't.

Taking the dress, Angel's Breath, from the box, Lily reverently hung it in her closet. She wouldn't wear this dress for anyone but Jake. It was the most beautiful gown she'd ever owned and she'd treasure it for the rest of her life.

After checking the contents of her meager closet, Lily chose a midi-length straight black skirt and matching jacket with padded shoulders. She dressed hurriedly, taking time only to freshen her makeup and run a brush through the tangles in her long hair. A dab of cologne behind her ears and at the pulse points on the inside of her wrists added to the rushed feeling. She'd just finished when the doorbell chimed. It could have been the neighbor children who liked to visit her and Gram, but Lily knew it was probably Rick. A glance at her slim wristwatch confirmed that he was right on time.

Gram was introducing herself to Rick when Lily appeared.

"Lily." Rick was looking at her with sparkling, appreciative eyes and took a step toward her. Claiming both hands, he kissed her lightly on the cheek.

Lily had to resist wiping his touch from her face. She hadn't found it offensive, only wrong. It wasn't Jake who was kissing her and it felt unnatural. "Hello, Rick." She did her utmost to disguise her lack of enthusiasm.

Automatically, her gaze slid into the kitchen where Jake was standing, half expecting him to object to the light intimacy Rick implied with the kiss.

Rick's eyes followed hers. "Glad to see there's no ill effects from your fall, Carson."

"None." The one word was as abrupt as a pistol shot.

"I'll be home early," Lily told Gram, hoping to avoid a confrontation between the two men.

Rick's hand curved around the back of Lily's neck. "But not too early."

At the front door she turned to Jake. "Thank you for today."

He pretended not to hear her and strode into the kitchen. Lily's heart throbbed painfully at the proud figure he made with his rigid back and tense shoulder muscles. He didn't like her going out with Rick, but he hadn't said a word.

"Jake doesn't mind you dating me, does he?" Rick asked when they reached his car. He drove a Mercedes 450 SL. Lily had often dreamed of riding in this type of convertible with the top down and the wind whipping through her thick hair. Now, when she was standing in front of one, she somehow couldn't muster up the appropriate enthusiasm.

"No, he doesn't mind," she told Rick.

"I don't want to horn in on you two if you've got something going. But from what Jake said . . ."

"There's nothing between us," Lily said, fighting the heavy sadness that permeated her voice. "We're only friends." *And then some*, she added silently. But the *some* hadn't been defined.

"Did I tell you where we were going?" Rick asked next, politely opening the car door for her.

"No."

"The Canlis."

Her returning smile was weak. "Thanks. Sounds fantastic."

They arrived at the popular restaurant a half-hour later. From everything she'd read, Lily knew the Canlis was highly rated and extremely expensive. For the first time she'd have the opportunity to order almond-saffron soup. Funny, now that the time had arrived, she'd have given almost anything to sit at the kitchen table across from Gram and Jake and struggle with the chopsticks Jake insisted they use to eat pork-fried rice.

"You have heard of the Canlis?" Rick wanted to know.

"Oh, yes. From what I understand, the food's wonderful."

"Only the best for you, Lily. Only the best."

Rick escorted Lily out for two evenings straight. On Sunday night, following their dinner at the Canlis, he took her to the Cliff House and ordered French champagne at a hundred dollars a bottle. After years of scrimping by with Gram for the bare necessities, Lily discovered her sense of priorities was offended by seeing good money wasted on something as frivolous as French wine.

When she mentioned it to Gram later, her grandmother simply shook her head. "Was it worth twenty dollars a glass?"

"That's the problem," Lily admitted, and sighed dejectedly. "I don't know. I've tasted champagne at least that good at a fraction of the cost."

"Rick must want to impress you."

Lily's gaze fell to her lap. "I think he does." Rick wined and dined her and claimed he found her utterly refreshing. He called her his "sunbeam" and was kind and patient. Lily should have been in ecstasy to have someone like Rick interested in her. She liked him, enjoyed his company and looked forward to seeing him again; but something basic was missing in their relationship—something that Lily couldn't quite put her finger on, but which was nonetheless essential.

On Monday evening Jake was waiting outside the Wheaton for her as usual. A warm smile lit up Lily's dark eyes as she stood in the hotel foyer and scanned the driveway. She spotted him quickly, standing outside his taxi.

"Hello, Jake," she said, walking toward him, her heart pounding crazily.

"Lily." He uncrossed his long legs and slowly straightened. "How'd it go tonight?"

"Good." About as good as it ever got, playing the same songs night after night.

"Meet any more rich Texans?" He forced the joke when the last thing he felt was witty.

"Not tonight."

"How did everything go with Rick?" Jake had thought of little else over the past two days. It felt good to be responsible for giving Lily what she wanted most. And wretched because it went against his instincts. But Rick was a decent sort. He'd be good to Lily.

"Rick's very nice."

"I knew you'd like him."

"I do." But not nearly as much as I like you, she added silently.

"Where'd he take you?"

"We went out to dinner."

"Canlis?"

"Yes. How did you know?"

"Rick always did have excellent taste." Most especially in women, Jake thought to himself. His friend wasn't going to let Lily slip away. She was a priceless gem, rare and exquisite, and it hadn't taken Rick long to discover her unspoiled beauty. Jake couldn't regret having introduced them; he'd planned it. Everything was turning out exactly as he wanted. But he hadn't expected that letting Lily go would be so damn difficult.

"How'd the writing go today?"

"Pretty good. I've got a story for you to read when you have the time." He reached inside the cab for a manila envelope and handed it to her.

Pleased, Lily hugged it to her breast. "Is there anything special you want me to look for?"

"The usual."

"Have you heard anything back on that one you sent to the *New Yorker*?"

Jake snickered and shook his head. "Lily, I only sent it there to please you. Trust me, the *New Yorker* isn't going to be interested in a story from me."

"Don't be such a defeatist. Who can say? That story was your best. I like it."

The corner of his mouth edged up in a self-mocking grimace. "You like all my stories."

"You're good, Jake. I just wish..."

"What?" He opened the passenger side for her and walked around the front of the vehicle.

"I think you ought to think about novels," Lily told him, once he was seated beside her.

"Maybe someday," he grumbled.

The evening traffic was lighter than usual as Jake drove the normal route to the Sunset district and Gram's. They didn't talk much after Lily suggested Jake consider writing novels. Ideas buzzed through his mind. Maybe he ought to think about it. Almost always the characters in his stories were strong enough to carry a book-length work. Naturally it would call for more plot development, and that could be a problem, but one he could work at learning. To his surprise, he found the idea appealing. He should probably try writing longer fiction. It couldn't hurt.

Lily studied the man sitting on the seat beside her. His gaze was centered on the street, his dark-green eyes narrowed in concentration. Sensing Lily's gaze on him, Jake turned his head toward her.

"Are you coming in tonight?"

Mentally Jake weighed the pros and cons. He liked talking over his day with Lily and Gram. They offered him an outlet to the everyday frustrations of life. Yet, coming around every night the way he used to could mean problems. The day they'd gone shopping proved that. But, hell, why should he worry? Gram was around.

"If you don't mind?"

Lily laughed, surprised that he'd even suggest such a thing. "Of course I don't mind. You're always welcome. You know that."

He smiled then until the emerald light sparkled in his eyes and Lily discovered she couldn't look away. His eyes held her as effectively as a vise.

"Yes, I guess I do at that," he said finally.

By the time Jake returned it was after eleven. Lily sat in the living room with Gram. She'd read over Jake's short story and made several markings on the manuscript. Every time she read something of Jake's she was stirred by the powerful use of emotion in his stories. This one was particularly impassioned. The story involved a strong, independent old man who lived alone. The man didn't like women or kids, but he had a soft spot in his heart for animals. Late one night, the crotchety old man found a lost dog that had been frightened and had nearly drowned in a bad storm. He brought the dog, a miniature French poodle, into his home and fed it cat food. As he worked at drying off the dog, he complained gruffly that Miss

Fifi deserved to be left out in the storm. The French poodle ignored the surly voice and looked up at him adoringly with deep, dark eyes. The little dog was so grateful to have been rescued that she insisted on following the old man around the house. Soon she was sleeping on the end of his bed and working her way into his crusty old heart. The old man would scowl at the dog and called her crude names, but the dog was content. People who saw the man with the fancy poodle were amused by the two. The old man wasn't sure what he felt for the dog. Miss Fifi was a damn nuisance and he sure as hell didn't like people snickering behind his back. Yet every day he grew more attached to the dog. At the end of the story he found her a good home and, without a second thought, went about his life as before.

Lily was sitting on the sofa with her feet tucked up under her when Jake knocked once and let himself inside.

His gaze fell to the manila envelope. "You're finished already?"

"Yes."

Gram was swaying in her rocker, watching the late-night newscast. She acknowledged Jake and returned her attention to the television set.

"Well?" He shouldn't have let her read it. Lily was frowning. The story wasn't one of his best. He should have ditched it. He sat on the end of the coffee table and leaned forward, resting his elbows on his knees.

"You're getting better and better," she hedged. "The best thing about your writing, Jake, is that you're a natural storyteller."

"But." He recognized that she was leading up to something unpleasant. He could tell by the dark frown that pinched her brow and by the way her eyes avoided his. Damn, he wished she wouldn't wear T-shirts.

"But . . . the ending's wrong in this one."

"What?" Jake's jaw sagged with surprise. He expected anything but that.

"The little dog loved that lonely old man."

"He wasn't lonely."

"But he was!" Lily protested. "That's the reason the old man came to love the dog so much. He longed for companionship."

"You're thinking like a woman again. The old man liked his life. He was content. He didn't need anyone or anything."

"But he loved that fancy dog."

"And people laughed at him." He found his gaze centered on her breasts again and damned himself for being so weak.

"Why should he care what people think? He didn't like them anyway. You've set him up to be an antisocial sort of fellow. The only friend he's got is this fancy dog."

Smiling sadly, Jake shook his head. "That crusty old man knows that fancy dog isn't right for him. He's doing the only thing he can by giving her to someone who will appreciate and love her."

"*He* appreciates and loves her," Lily countered hotly.

"But he isn't right for her. And by finding her a good home, he's revealing the strength of his love."

"Ha! That's not strength. If anything, he's showing how weak he is to give in to the opinion of others."

Jake got up and rubbed a hand over his eyes. "You missed the point of the story."

"I didn't miss it," Lily told him shortly. "It's right here, hitting me between the eyes. That old man, who you wanted the reader to see as strong and fiercely proud, was actually shallow and foolish."

"Shallow and foolish!" Jake almost flung the words back at her. "He's noble and unselfish." Something was wrong with Lily that she could take this short story and entirely miss the point. Normally he sought her feedback, but this time she was entirely off base. The old man was a classic tragic hero. Literature had rarely sported a finer one. It astonished him that Lily, who was normally so intuitive, couldn't see that.

"Let's agree to disagree," he proposed.

"It won't sell, Jake."

"So?" He fought down a ready argument. "I've got tons of stories that'll never see a printed page."

"But this one could, if you'd change the plot around."

"I'm not changing a damn thing."

"That's your choice then." She folded her arms over her chest and stared past him to the picture on the wall. In the past Jake had taken what she felt about a story to heart. Usually he made the changes she suggested and showed his appreciation for her insight and good judgment.

"You're right about one thing: it is my choice." He couldn't believe Lily had missed the most important lesson in the short piece.

A heavy silence settled over them.

"Would you like a glass of Marmite?" Lily asked five minutes later, seeking some way to smooth matters over. She was uncomfortable when things weren't right between her and Jake.

"Sure." Jake followed her into the kitchen. "You disappoint me, Lily."

"I do?" She hesitated before returning the teakettle to the stove. "How?"

"With the story. You're thinking like a woman and forgetting that this is a man's story."

"Women buy the majority of magazines."

"Maybe."

"Maybe nothing—that's hard fact. And what's so wrong with thinking like a woman? In case you hadn't noticed, I *am* one."

Oh, he'd noticed all right. Every time she moved in that silly T-shirt, he noticed. From the instant he'd walked in the door, her breasts had enthralled him. They were pressed against the thin material of her shirt, round and full. At first he suspected that she wasn't wearing a bra, and was about to chastise her. But soon it became apparent that she was and he struggled to look elsewhere. Yet again and again, against the very fiber of his will, his gaze was lured back to her. He knew if he were to hold her, her breast would fill his palm, overflow his hand. If he were to taste her breasts... Oh, dear Lord, what a thought! She'd be incomparable. Everything about Lily was perfection.

Stalking to the other side of the room, Jake swallowed tightly and forced his gaze in the opposite direction.

"The fact is," Lily continued, "I don't much like your 'classic' hero."

"I thought we were through discussing the story."

"You were the one who brought it up."

"My mistake." Jake ground his teeth in an effort to hold her eye and not allow his gaze to drop.

"What are you two shouting about?" Gram asked, joining them.

"Jake's story."

"Nothing," Jake countered, and at her fiery gaze, he added, "I thought we agreed not to discuss it."

"Fine." Lily's arms hugged her waist.

"You two sound like snapping turtles."

"We aren't going to argue anymore, Gram," Lily promised.

"The way you two have been carrying on lately, one would think you were married. Me and Paddy sounded just like the two of you. We'd fight, but then we'd make up, too. Those were the best times," she chuckled. "Oh, yes, making up was the best part."

"We aren't fighting," Lily insisted.

"And there isn't a snowball's chance in hell that we'd ever marry," Jake barked angrily.

Involuntarily, Lily winced. She was surprised that Jake's words would have the power to hurt her. "You aren't exactly my idea of good husband material, either."

"Of course I'm not," Jake growled. "You're like every other female—you want someone who can run a four-minute mile after a fast buck."

"And what's wrong with that? The way Gram and I have lived...we deserve something better. At least I'm honest." With everything that was in her, Lily battled to hold on to her temper. She paused to take in several deep breaths. "Maybe it would be best if I didn't read your stories anymore, Jake."

"You're right about that," he declared, marching into the living room. He jerked the manila envelope off the coffee table with such force he nearly knocked the table over. "Damn right," he said again on his way out the front door.

The screen door slammed and Lily cringed, closing her eyes.

"You two sound like Paddy and me," Gram announced a second time.

Lily's answering smile was feeble and nearly nonexistent. She and Jake weren't anything like Gram and Paddy. Her grandparents shared a mutual trust and a love so rare and true that it had spanned even death.

Unshed tears brightened Lily's eyes as she slowly walked through the house and turned off the lights one by one.

The next evening Jake wasn't outside the Wheaton when Lily was finished at the piano. Standing in the lobby she looked out at the long circular driveway and sighed her disappointment. She'd hoped they would have a chance to talk. But Jake was angry, probably angrier than he'd ever been with her. Lily couldn't stand it. Their friendship was too important to let something as petty as a short story stand between them.

Dejectedly, Lily secured her purse strap over her shoulder and walked into the cool evening air. Her thoughts were troubled and she felt as if she carried the weight of a grand piano on her back. She was at the end of the long driveway when she recognized Jake's cab barreling down the street. He eased to a stop at her side along the curb.

Lily couldn't hide the way her heart leaped at the sight of him. Her dark, anguished gaze sought his.

Jake leaned across the front seat and opened the door. "Are you talking to me?"

"Of course."

"Climb in and I'll give you a ride home."

Lily didn't hesitate. "Jake..."

"No, let me go first. I apologize. You were right about the story. I don't know what was wrong with me."

"No," she contradicted in a hurried breath. "I was the one who was wrong. I've felt wretched all day. We shouldn't fight."

"No, we shouldn't." He grinned at her then—that crooked, sexy grin of his that melted her insides—and reached for her hand, squeezing her fingers. "Let's agree to disagree," Jake suggested.

Lily smiled and felt the tension of twenty hours drain from her. "What did you do with the story?"

"Threw it out."

"But Jake, it was a good story. With a few changes, I know it would sell."

"Maybe. But I wasn't willing to change the ending. The best place for it was the trash can."

"I wish you hadn't." For some inexplicable reason, having Jake discard the story depressed her.

"Friends?" he questioned.

"Friends." Jake may have thrown away the story, but they'd learned something about each other in the process. Their friendship was important. The world wasn't right when they were at odds with each other. Whatever else happened, they couldn't discard what they shared.

The melancholy feeling persisted as Jake drove her home. She bid him goodnight and raced up the walk toward the house.

"Rick called," Gram told Lily when she walked in the front door.

"Okay." Lily stood at the window, watching Jake drive away. "Jake and I are friends again."

"Were you enemies before?"

"No, but we had a fight and now that's over."

"And you fretted about it most of the day."

"I was worried," Lily corrected, releasing the drape so that it fell against the window. "I don't feel right when there's something wrong between Jake and me."

"I know what you mean. I felt the same way when Paddy and I fought."

Lily remained at the window long after Jake had driven out of sight. Rick was waiting for her to phone back and Gram was walking around comparing Lily and Jake to her and Paddy. They weren't anything alike. Gram and Paddy were lovers who had traveled the world and lived through hair-raising adventures. Jake and Lily were friends...and then some, her mind echoed...and then some.

"Gram, how do I look?" Lily had swirled her hair high atop her head and put on the ruby dress.

"As pretty as a picture," Gram confirmed without looking up from the crossword puzzle she was working on.

"Gram, you didn't even look."

"But you're always pretty. You don't need me to tell you that." She yawned loudly, covering her red lips with one veined hand. "You seeing Rick or Jake tonight?"

"Rick." She hoped the lack of enthusiasm wasn't evident in her voice.

"You don't sound pleased about it."

It did show. "We're going to the opera."

"You'll love that."

Lily had dreamed of attending such an affair most of her life. Rick had managed to obtain tickets to Mozart's *Così Fan Tutte*, which was being performed by the Metropolitan Opera Company from New York. From what little Lily knew, the performance had been sold out for months. She didn't know how Rick had managed it. He'd mentioned it once and her eyes had lit up with unrestrained eagerness and the next thing she knew, he had two tickets.

"It's something I've always wanted to do," Lily agreed. She yearned to study the gowns the women wore and see their jewels. Rick was kind and generous. He'd be the type of husband who would take pleasure in buying his wife huge diamonds and clothing her in mink. Lily forced a smile to her lips. Those things had been important to her for so long, she hated the thought of doing without them. But Rick deserved so much more than what she could give him. He deserved someone who would love him and be his friend.

The sound of footsteps pounding up the cement walkway directed Lily's attention to the front of the house.

"Lily!" Jake burst in the front door and grabbed her by the waist. His handsome face was flushed with pleasure and his emerald eyes sparked with an energy and excitement Lily had never seen.

"A letter from the *New Yorker* came today. They want my story!"

"Oh, Jake!" Squealing with delight and laughing, she threw her arms around his neck and gleefully tossed back her head.

Hugging her, Jake lifted her from the carpet and whirled around and around until they were both dizzy and weak.

"The best part of the whole thing is the money they're paying me." He set her back on the carpet but kept his arms around her waist. Holding Lily greatly increased the excitement that soared through his blood. Nor did her hands leave his shoulders as she smiled up at him, her eyes filled with warmth and happiness.

"I knew it would sell," she told him. "I knew it."

Jake knew he had to either let go of Lily or pull her to him and sample anew her sweet kiss. Reluctantly, he chose the former and turned to Gram who was sitting in her old rocker, swaying.

"Nzuri sana," Gram cried, resorting to the happy Swahili word to express her congratulations.

Jake bent down and kissed the older woman soundly on the cheek. "We're celebrating. All three of us. A night on the town, dinner, dancing. Wine, women, song. No more beer and television for us."

Lily's heart sank all the way to her knees. "When?"

"Right now." Jake paused, seeming to notice her dress for the first time, and sobered. "You're going somewhere." There was no question in his voice. He knew. The rare joy bubbling inside him quickly went flat and stale.

"To the opera with..."

"...Rick," he finished for her. He rammed both hands into his pants pockets and gestured outwardly with his elbows. "Listen, that's not a problem. We'll do it another time."

"I don't want to do it another time."

"It works out this way sometimes," Jake announced. "Don't worry about it." He headed out the door.

"Gram?" Lily turned frustrated, unhappy eyes to her grandmother and cried. "What should I do?"

"That's up to you, girl," Gram answered obliquely, continuing to rock and work the crossword puzzle.

"Jake—" As fast as her long, straight skirt would allow, Lily rushed out the door after Jake. "Wait up." The screen slammed and Lily hurried down the stairs of the porch.

Jake paused in front of his cab, car keys in his hand. "What?" He centered his gaze on the keys in the palm of his hand.

"Don't go," she pleaded.

"From the look of you, Rick will be here any minute."

"Yes, but I want to go with you."

"I've heard you talk for an entire year about attending an opera. You're going. We'll celebrate another time."

"But I want to be with you."

"No."

Lily battled with herself. She couldn't wait. They deserved this time together. This sale was their victory, their triumph. Ever so briefly, Jake had held her with an exhilaration that would fade in time. She wanted to be with him tonight more than anything— more than seeing an opera or sharing almond-saffron soup with Rick.

"Please, please come back in three hours," she pleaded, holding his hand. "I'll be waiting for you."

Because she couldn't stop herself, Lily stood on tiptoes and planted a hot, heartfelt kiss on the side of his mouth.

Chapter Six

"Are you sure you're going to be all right?" Rick asked with such tender concern Lily thought she might cry.

In response, she pressed her palms against her stomach and leaned her head against the headrest in the luxury car. "I'm sure it's nothing serious."

"I should have known you weren't feeling well." Rick's gentle voice was tinged with self-derisive anger. "You haven't been yourself all evening."

Because Lily had felt guilty all evening!

"You've been so quiet."

It wasn't like her to deceive anyone!

"I only wish you'd said something earlier."

She couldn't. When she had asked Rick to take her home because she wasn't well, Lily had felt as if there were a neon light that identified her as a scheming liar flashing on her forehead.

When Rick parked the Mercedes in front of Gram's, Lily automatically looked around for Jake's cab. She saw no sign of it and didn't know whether to be grateful or increasingly depressed.

Smoothly Rick climbed out of the car and crossed over to her side, opening her door. He gave her his hand and studied her with worried eyes. "You're so pale. Are you sure you don't want me to stay with you?"

"No," she cried quickly, perhaps too quickly. "But thank you, dear Rick, for being so good to me." Her lashes fluttered against the high arch of her cheek as she dismally cast her gaze to the sidewalk.

"I want to be good to you for a very long time," Rick announced softly, tenderly slipping an arm around her waist and guiding her toward the house. "I never hoped to find someone as good as you, Lily."

The stomach ailment Lily had invented became increasingly more real. Her insides knotted with painful reality. They paused on the porch and Rick tucked a finger under her chin, raising her eyes to his. Ever so gently, he brushed his mouth over her cheek. "Can I see you next week?"

Lily would have agreed to anything if it would help lessen her intense feeling of guilt. "If you'd like."

"Oh, I'd like, my sunbeam, I'd like it very much." With that he tenderly lifted the hair from her forehead and kissed her again.

Lily felt all the physical response of a rag doll. She didn't lift her hands to his shoulders or encourage him, but Rick didn't appear to care or notice.

"I'll phone you in the morning," he promised. Within a minute, he was gone.

Like a soldier returning to camp after a long day of exhausting maneuvers, Lily walked into the house. Gram was asleep and snoring in her rocking chair. The crossword puzzle had slipped unnoticed to the floor. Gently, Lily shook her grandmother.

"Come on, Gram, let me help you into bed."

Gram jerked awake with a start. "Oh, it's you."

"Who were you expecting?"

"Jake. You did say he was coming back, didn't you?"

"Yes . . . but he isn't here."

"He will be," Gram stated confidently, sitting upright. She rubbed a hand over her eyes and looked around her as though half expecting Jake to be there without either of them noticing. "Trust me, girl, he'll be here."

Lily wasn't as certain. He hadn't agreed to her scheme, but he hadn't told her outright that he wouldn't be back either. He'd known from the beginning that the sale of this short story was their success. Lily had been the one to convince Jake to submit it to the *New Yorker*. They'd *agreed* on this one.

While Gram was rambling around the living room, Lily changed out of her evening gown and into the white dress that Jake had bought her. A night as significant as this one demanded a dress that was just as special.

Pausing at her bedroom window, Lily parted the drape and stared into the starlit sky. The street was empty and her heart throbbed with anticipation. If Jake didn't come, she didn't know what she'd do. Perhaps go to his boat. Tonight he wouldn't escape her.

A half-hour later, Lily sat in the still living room, staring silently ahead at the moonlight flickering against the elephant tusks that adorned the wall. The moving shadows seemed to taunt and tease her for being so foolish.

Gram's last words before heading to bed were that Jake would come. It was after eleven now and so silent, Lily imagined that death must feel like this. What morbid thoughts! She shook her head, mentally chastising herself.

The sound of Jake's cab registered in her mind and she bolted to her feet, sucked in a calming breath and rushed to the door. He had come.

Anxiously she was standing on the porch by the time he'd parked. He didn't look eager to see her and stopped the instant he realized she was wearing the dress. When he started toward her again, he trod heavily—like someone being led to a labor camp.

"Gram said you'd come." She rubbed her hands together to chase away the unexpected chill of uncertainty.

Jake spread his fingers wide in a gesture that told her he hadn't wanted to return. But something stronger than his will had led him back to her.

"What did you tell Rick?" He stood on the sidewalk as if he weren't quite certain yet that he wanted inside.

"That I wasn't feeling well."

"And he bought that?"

"By the time we left the opera it was true."

"And how are you feeling now?"

"Terrible." She hung her head so that her hair fell forward and formed a wreath about her tight features. Lily continued to rub her palms against each other.

"I shouldn't be here." Why did Lily have to look so beautiful standing there in the moonlight? She was miserable and confused and it took everything in him not to reach for her and haul her into his arms and comfort her. Rick had probably wanted to do that. Involuntarily, Jake's fist clenched. The thought of Rick holding and touching Lily produced such a rage within him that he felt like smashing his clenched hand through a wall. Well, he'd better get used to it.

"I'm glad you came," Lily said softly, hesitatingly.

Her intense young face commanded his attention. She was pale and so lovely surrounded by the moonlight that he would grant her anything if she asked. Her eyes held his, wide and inquiring, and Jake knew he could refuse her nothing.

"I'm glad I did too," he admitted with reluctance, walking toward her.

"It's a little late for going out to eat. I thought . . . that is, if you don't mind . . . that we could order a pizza."

"With anchovies?"

Her eyes lit up with a teasing glint. "Only on your half."

"Agreed." He took the stairs two at a time and paused at the darkened living room. "Where's Gram?"

"She fell asleep. I'll wake her."

"No." A hand on Lily's forearm stopped her. No, tonight was for them. "Let her rest."

"All right."

She smiled at him and Jake felt his stomach twist. Dear Lord, she was lovely. If he had any sense left, he'd get out of there right away. But the ability to reason had left him the first time he'd kissed Lily that night in the attic. From that minute on he'd behaved like a besotted fool. He didn't like the feeling. Elaine had made a simpleton out of him. He'd like to blame Lily for what he was feeling, but he couldn't. With her, everything had been of his own making.

"I bought some wine." Actually it was in the front seat of the cab. He hadn't brought it with him because he hadn't been sure he'd be staying. "I'll be right back."

Lily had the wineglasses down by the time he returned. She turned to him when he walked into the kitchen and Jake found himself mesmerized anew by her. He couldn't look away from her no matter how hard he tried. The shape of her mouth intrigued him, the delicate curve of her cheek, the soulful dark eyes that regarded him with trust and innocence.

"Do you want a corkscrew?"

Lily's words shook him. "Yeah, sure." He paused to clear his throat. "You look nice in that dress." That had to be the understatement of the year. She was the image of the very name of the gown: Angel's Breath— all soft and womanly so that it was the purest form of torture to be near her and not touch her.

Lily handed him the corkscrew and while he fiddled with the cork in the narrow neck of the wine bottle, she flipped through the pages of the telephone directory. "Should we pick the pizza up ourselves or have it delivered?"

"That's up to you."

"Have it delivered." Lily didn't want to go out again or do anything that would disrupt this evening. "What toppings do you want?"

"Anchovies, pepperoni, olives, green pepper—" he paused "—and sausage. What about you?"

"Cheese," she told him, and laughed at the funny look that came over him. "I'm just teasing. I'll have everything you order except those disgusting little fish."

The cork came out of the wine bottle with a popping sound and Jake filled both glasses. "Here."

Lily accepted the wine and took a small sip. It was excellent. "This is good."

"I wanted something special."

She touched the edge of her wineglass to his. "To Jake: a master of words, a skilled storyteller, a man of obvious talent and virtue."

"And to Lily, who lent me her support."

"Moral and immoral," she added with a small laugh.

"Mostly moral."

Together they tasted the wine. By unspoken mutual consent they moved into the living room and sat on the zebra skin beside the wide ottoman. For an instant Lily thought to suggest that they light a fire in the fireplace, but the evening was warm. The fire would have been more for atmosphere than for heat.

"Thank you, Lily, for your encouragement."

"Thank you, Jake, for being who you are."

"To friendship." His eyes didn't leave hers.

"To friendship," she repeated in a hushed whisper.

Companionably, they drank the first glass and Jake replenished their supply.

"Jake."

"Hmm?"

"What really happened between you and Elaine?"

The question came at him from outer space and was so unexpected that his mouth sagged open. "What do you want to know for?"

She lifted one shoulder and lowered her gaze to the red liquid. "You were so close to her."

"Yeah. So?"

"And then everything blew up."

"She wanted me to be something I couldn't."

"But that's the most astonishing thing about you, Jake. You're so versatile. You can do anything."

"But only if I want to." Jake had no qualms about his talents. He'd tried enough things in life to know what Lily said was true. He wasn't being egotistical in admitting as much, only honest.

With a lazy finger, Lily drew imaginary circles over the top of her wineglass. "Did you make love to her?"

"What?" Jake sat up so quickly that the wine nearly sloshed over the sides of his glass. "What kind of question is that?"

"I just wanted to know." Morbid curiosity had driven her to ask. Even the thought of Jake kissing Elaine was so painful, Lily could hardly breathe just imagining it.

"A lady has no business asking a man that kind of thing."

"Sorry... But did you?"

"That's none of your business." He downed the remainder of his glass in one giant swallow. "I hope this isn't the type of conversation you have with Rick."

Lily was aghast. "Of course not!"

"I should hope so." In that moment he couldn't even recall what Elaine looked like—or any other woman. His mind's eye was filled with Lily. He'd carry the picture of her standing on the porch waiting for him in that white dress for the rest of his life.

"I know you and Elaine were very close." Lily's eyes went hazy.

"Do you mind if we don't talk about Elaine? I'm sure there are a thousand other subjects far more suitable and fathoms more interesting."

"All right." Already Lily regretted having brought up the other woman. Jake had loved Elaine and been hurt by her. Given the opportunity, Lily would have liked to scratch out the other woman's eyes for disillusioning Jake. But Lily couldn't regret that they'd broken up. Elaine wasn't good enough for Jake.

"What about you and Rick?"

She straightened. "What about us?"

"Has he kissed you?"

Lily clamped her upper teeth over her bottom lip and hunched her shoulders. "Sort of."

"How does a man 'sort of' kiss you?"

Lily rose to her knees, planted her hands on his shoulders and slanted her mouth over Jake's. "Like this," she whispered, gently grazing his mouth with hers. Her touch was so light that their mouths barely touched in a whisper-soft caress.

Jake's immediate reaction was so profound that he nearly choked on his own breath. A shaft of desire shot through him so quickly he hadn't the time to question or analyze it. Quickly he broke the contact and leaned back, lowering his gaze. Her breasts were achingly close to his chest and she smelled like summer and sunshine and everything good. He had to look away, fearing that if he gazed at Lily a second longer, he'd toss aside the wineglass and drag her into his arms. "Yes, well, I see what you mean."

"You knew Rick was married before, didn't you?"

"I seem to remember something about that."

"He's been divorced less than a year."

"What happened?" Jake didn't care two cents about the breakup of Rick's marriage, but he needed to talk. Anything to take his mind off what sitting beside Lily was doing to him. He tried to avoid touching her, adjusting his position several times, but nothing was satisfactory and he finally settled so that just their knees brushed together.

"I'm not exactly sure, but apparently she left him for another man."

"That must've hurt." The remark was inane, but every second was torture having Lily so close.

"He's insecure and lonely."

"So are a lot of others."

Lily rotated the stem of the wineglass between her thumb and fingers. "I know."

"You like Rick, don't you?" Jake pressed. His gut feeling that Rick wasn't right for Lily persisted, but he wouldn't say anything. Not after the first time with that oil-rich Texan. Rick may not be sterling enough for Lily, but Jake was beginning to doubt that anyone was good enough.

"He's a nice man."

"Rich."

Softly, Lily cleared her throat. "Yes, he seems to be."

"That's what you wanted."

Lately, Lily wasn't so sure. She set the wineglass aside, got up, and moved to the window to stare into the night. The city lights obliterated the brilliance of the stars, but Lily was only pretending to look into the sky.

Jake joined her, coming to stand behind her. His chin touched the top of her head and he raised his hands to cup the gentle curve of her shoulders and rested his cheek against the side of her head. "It's a beautiful night, isn't it?" He shouldn't be touching her like this, even in the most innocent way. Her nearness was a stimulant he didn't need. And she felt warm and vital and smelled much too good for his sanity. Rick could give her all the things he'd never be able to afford. A knot of misery tightened in Jake's chest.

"Yes, it's lovely," she mumbled. Without meaning to, she leaned back against Jake. He accepted her weight and slid his hands down the length of her arms. Desperately he wanted to hold her without embracing her—to touch her without giving in to the overwhelming temptation to kiss her. Lily was meant to be cherished and treasured, and he couldn't do her justice. Maybe Rick could, but he doubted it.

Lily didn't move, barely breathed. The light touch of Jake's hands stirred her blood. She yearned to turn and have his arms surround her. The light taste of his mouth lingered on hers and she yearned for more than a tantalizing sample.

Involuntarily, Jake turned his face into her hair and breathed in the fragrance of her cologne. He lowered his face and nuzzled her ear. Lily tilted her head, luxuriating in the hot sensation that flooded through her.

"Lily," Jake breathed desperately. "I shouldn't be holding you like this."

"I like it."

"I do too. Too damn much. Tell me to stop."

"But I don't want you to."

"Lily, please."

"Don't hold me then," she murmured in the faintest of whispers. "Let me hold you." Without warning, she turned and slipped her arms around his waist and pressed her ear against his heart. The wild pounding tempo matched her own.

"Lily, don't do this."

"It feels good in your arms," she protested, tightening her grip so that he couldn't break the contact. "How can it be wrong when it feels this good?"

"I don't know. Oh, Lily..." He whispered her name in a low guttural sound as he lowered his head, searching out her mouth. He touched his lips against hers, sampling them, savoring the feel and unique flavor of her. She tasted like melting sugar, unbearably sweet and highly addictive.

Restlessly she moved against him, rubbing her upper torso to him, seeking what she didn't know. A release? More of his touch?

"Lily," he pleaded against her mouth. "Hold still. Please, don't move."

"I can't help it." Arching against him, her breasts grazed his chest and Jake groaned like a man being tortured. Using a power she hadn't realized she possessed, she combed her fingers through his hair and looked up at him with wide, adoring eyes. She brushed her hips against him and Jake shut his eyes, fighting back his body's natural response.

"Lily..."

"Shh," she whispered and planted her lips over his. She gave him a glimpse of heaven, winding her arms around his neck and caressing his mouth with hers. "You taste good."

"Oh Lord, so do you." He paused to study the innocence of her gaze and called himself every kind of idiot. They were playing a dangerous game at which they would both turn up losers. Yet he was unable to resist her and he lowered his mouth to capture hers again.

Lily whimpered, rubbing her lips back and forth over his in the lightest, soul-stirring caress known. A low moaning sound slipped from Jake's throat and he forced a deeper contact, gripping the sides of her face and fusing their mouths together.

He came away from her weak, his resolve diminishing by the second. He hugged her hard, struggling deep within himself to find the willpower to walk away. He had no right to touch and kiss Lily that way. No right. He gnashed his teeth in an effort to win back his control.

With a superhuman effort, he broke the contact, pushing her away and holding her at arm's length. "The wine went to our heads."

Her small smile contradicted his words. "We didn't have that much."

"Obviously more than we should have."

"I like what you do to me."

"Well, I don't like it," he whispered fiercely. "Tonight was a fluke and best forgotten."

"I'm not going to forget it."

"Well, I am. This isn't going to happen again. Do you understand? It's not right."

"But Jake . . ."

"I'm leaving. Right now, while the gettin's good. If you have half the intelligence I credit you with, you'll forget this unfortunate incident ever happened." He dropped his arms, and rubbed a hand over his face. "Goodnight, Lily."

She could hardly see him. Salty tears clouded her vision. "Goodnight, Jake," she whispered miserably. He was gone before she could utter another word.

"Morning." Gram greeted Lily cheerfully the following day. "I see Jake came. I told you he would."

Lily pulled out a kitchen chair and absently reached for one of Gram's vitamin tablets. After a sleepless, restless, unhappy night she felt the need for some fabricated energy.

"Yes, he was here."

"You coming down with a cold, girl? Your eyes are all red like you were awake half the night."

Lily blinked and offered her grandmother a feeble smile. "I think I might be."

Gram pushed a handful of tablets in Lily's direction. "You better start taking these."

"All right."

Gram gave her an odd look as Lily downed each capsule without argument. "I see you two celebrated with some wine."

"Jake brought it." Her explanation was mumbled.

"Where'd he take you for dinner?"

They had never gotten around to ordering the pizza. "We . . . we just had the wine."

"Ah," Gram muttered knowingly. "So you sat around and talked."

Lily pulled out the chair and stood in front of the old porcelain sink, her back to her grandmother. "Yes, we talked." Her fingers tightened around her mug. They'd talked, and a lot more. It was the 'lot more' that would be difficult to explain.

"What did Jake have to say?"

"This and that." Nervously, Lily set the mug on the long counter. "I think I'll go get dressed."

"You do that," Gram said with a knowing chuckle. "Me and Paddy used to talk about 'this and that' ourselves. Some of our best conversations were spent discussing those very things—'this and that.'"

On Monday evening Jake wasn't parked in his usual spot outside the Wheaton when Lily finished her shift. She made an excuse to linger around the lobby for an additional fifteen minutes, hoping he'd arrive so they'd have the chance to talk. He didn't. And he wasn't there the next evening, either. Lily didn't require a typed message to know that Jake was avoiding her. Maybe Jake felt they needed a break from each other to give ample thought to what had happened. But Lily would have felt better if Jake hadn't been playing a silly game of hide-and-seek with her.

Early Wednesday evening, Rick appeared in the lobby of the Wheaton and sat listening to Lily play. He clapped politely at the end of a series of numbers. No one applauded her playing; she was there for mood and atmosphere, not as entertainment.

When she had finished, Lily slid off the polished piano bench and Rick rose to join her.

"You're very gifted," he said, kissing her on the cheek.

"Thank you."

"Would you like a cocktail?"

Lily hesitated. She wanted to check if Jake was out front. She'd been waiting hours for the opportunity to see if he were there. If he was, Lily had everything she wanted to tell him worked out in her mind. She had no intention of mentioning what had happened over the wine. She'd decided that she'd play Jake's game and pretend the alcohol had dictated their uncharacteristic behavior. She planned to be witty and clever and show him that she hadn't been nearly as affected by his kiss as he seemed to believe. Playing this role was a matter of pride now. "Let me tell Jake first," Lily told Rick.

"Sure." A guiding hand at her elbow led her through the hotel and into the huge foyer. "Why do you need to talk to Jake?"

"He usually gives me a ride home."

"Every night?" A faint sound of disapproval coated Rick's voice. "I wasn't aware that you saw Jake that often."

"That's how we got to be such good friends." Lily stood between the two sets of thick glass doors, scanning the long circular driveway. Jake wasn't there. Her heart sank and disappointment settled over her like a heavy, rain-sodden cloak.

"Apparently he can't tonight."

"Apparently not."

"I'll take you home. For that matter, there isn't any reason why I can't see you home every night. I hate the thought of you having to rely on Jake's schedule for a ride home."

"I'm not relying on Jake's schedule. He's here when he can be, and not here when it's inconvenient or he's got a fare. The agreement works well for us both." Perhaps she did depend more on Jake than she should. But Jake would be as offended as she to have Rick suggest as much. "And as for you seeing me home every night, that's ridiculous."

"But I want to take care of you," Rick protested, his arm closing around her waist. "Let's go have that drink and we'll talk it over."

"There's nothing to discuss." Now Rick was irritating her. She didn't want to have a drink with him; she wanted to talk to Jake. Only Jake wasn't around and hadn't been for three days. Lily missed him so much and felt so uncertain that she didn't know how to react. She hadn't realized how much she shared with Jake—nonsensical things about her day that only he would understand.

By Saturday afternoon, Lily was irritable and snapping at Gram. Rick had declared that he was coming to listen to her again and Jake continued to avoid her. Lily couldn't recall a time in all her years when she felt more frustrated with life.

"I haven't seen Jake around this week," Gram complained as Lily pulled weeds from the front flower beds. Two neighborhood children had stopped off earlier for a visit and Lily had baked cookies with them while Gram told them stories about Africa.

Now Gram groomed her African violets with the secret smile she got when she talked about her adventures in the "dark continent" with Paddy. She wore a huge straw hat that was connected to a brightly colored bandanna that tied under her chin.

"Jake hasn't been around." With unnecessary force she jerked a weed free of the soft soil. "I haven't seen him an entire week."

"Not since you two discussed 'this and that'?" Gram asked with a thoughtful glance.

"Nope." The cool earth felt good against Lily's hands. For once she didn't care if there was grit and grime under her carefully manicured nails. And if she had to play "Moon River" one more time, she swore she'd croak. "Gram, what would you say about me changing jobs?"

"Changing jobs? But I thought you liked it at the Wheaton. Or is it Jake that's worrying you?"

"Jake hasn't got anything to do with it."

"This decision seems sudden."

"Forget it, then. I'll stay at the Wheaton and play 'Moon River' for the rest of my life. I simply don't care if I ever see Jake again." The minute the words escaped her lips, Lily realized what she'd said, and snapped her mouth closed.

"Seems to me that you're more worried about seeing Jake than you are about playing that song."

Rather than comment, Lily pressed her lips closed. She had already said more than she'd intended.

"I don't know that there's any rule against you going to see him," Gram continued, undaunted. "It seems to me that in this day and age a woman has a right to pay a man a visit if she likes."

"Should I?" Lily hesitated. Her first inclination was to hurry to the marina, but she had her pride to consider. Already it had taken a beating, and Lily doubted that it would go another round.

"I can't see what harm it'd do."

To Lily's burdened mind it could solve several problems. To hell with her pride! "Maybe I will drop by and see how he is. He might be ill or something."

"He could even be waiting for you to come."

Lily sat back on her haunches and brushed a stray curl from her face. A thin layer of mud smeared her cheek. "Do you honestly think he's waiting?"

"I can't rightly say, but it wouldn't do any harm to find out."

By the time Lily had showered, changed clothes and dressed casually in jeans and a T-shirt, she was nervous and fidgety. Maybe going to Jake's wasn't the best idea, but Lily couldn't stand the terrible silence any longer.

On her way to the marina, she stopped off at Shankey's and ordered the pizza they hadn't gotten around to eating that other night. Carrying the thin cardboard box in both hands, Lily walked down the long, rolling dock to where his sailboat was moored.

"Jake!" Her voice trembled as she called out his name.

Below deck, Jake heard the sound of Lily's voice and shoved the story he was typing into the cutlery drawer.

Chapter Seven

Lily's voice had gone through Jake like a laser, searing his senses. He got up slowly, unsure of what he should do. He'd avoided her all week and with good cause. After what had happened at their "victory celebration," they should have sense enough to stay away from each other.

Besides, he reasoned, Lily didn't need him anymore; she had Rick. Jake knew that Rick had been at the Wheaton every evening. After all this time, he still couldn't reconcile himself to Lily's dating Rick. But hell, he'd introduced them, set them up and gone out of his way to arrange their meeting. He couldn't very well announce to Lily that she shouldn't continue seeing Rick. That rich lawyer wasn't good enough for her. But then, Jake sincerely doubted that anyone was. Jake was snared in a trap of his own making. The best thing for him to do was make himself scarce.

"Jake, I know you're in there." Lily called again.

Impatiently, Jake's fist clenched at his side and an irritated noise slipped from deep inside his throat. If he didn't react it would be just like that stubborn woman to hop on board the *Lucky Lady* and search him out. Then he'd look like even more of a fool than he did already. Reluctantly he climbed on deck.

"Hello, Jake," Lily began awkwardly.

He tucked in his shirttails, giving the impression that he'd been preoccupied. "Lily."

"Did I catch you at a bad time? You weren't asleep, were you? Gram thought you might be sick."

His gaze just managed to avoid hers. "This is a bit of a bad moment. I'm busy."

"Oh." She dropped her gaze. "I brought a pizza. We...the other night we forgot about it."

"We didn't exactly forget it," he corrected her. "We just didn't get around to ordering it." He lifted his gaze and his eyes delved into hers. Dear heaven, she was beautiful, standing there with those huge brown eyes, looking as betrayed and hurt as a wounded fawn. Her woebegone expression was as seductive as her breasts arching against his chest and her lips trembling under his had been.

"Anyway, I thought I could bring a pizza now."

Determinedly Jake kept his gaze trained on the flat box in her arms.

"But if you're busy, I'll understand." She didn't, not really. He must realize that coming here had cost her a lot of pride. The least he could do was make it easier on her.

Something in her voice reminded Jake that this wasn't any less difficult for Lily. He couldn't protect his ego at her expense. "It was thoughtful of you to come."

The tension leaked from Lily's stiff back as Jake stretched out his hand to help her aboard. The boat rocked gently as she shifted her weight from the narrow dock to the *Lucky Lady*.

"There are anchovies on your half." She smiled up at him and Jake knew instantly that he was in trouble.

Lily drew in a long, languorous breath as though she didn't know what to say or do now that she was aboard the boat.

"It looks like rain, doesn't it?" Lily suggested, casting a discerning eye toward the thick gray clouds. "Maybe we should take this below."

The hard muscles of Jake's chest tightened. Being alone with Lily was bad enough, but being forced to stand or sit next to her in the close confines of the cabin was almost more than he could bear.

"Jake?"

"Yeah, sure." He led the way and Lily handed the pizza down to him before expertly maneuvering the few steps that led below deck.

"Have you been working on another story?" Lily asked as she spied his typewriter. Bunched-up pieces of paper littered the tabletop and filled what limited space there was in the dining area. "It looks like you're having a few problems. Do you want to tell me your plot? That helps, sometimes."

Setting the pizza beside the tiny sink, Jake made busy work of clearing away his mess. "No," he answered starkly.

Lily was shocked, too stunned to react quickly. For a tension-filled minute neither spoke.

"Why not?" Jake often talked out his plot ideas with her and listened to her reactions. Invariably, he argued his point and then, more often than not, accepted her suggestions.

"Every writer comes to the time when he has to break away..."

Lily heaved a giant sigh and shook her head sadly. "Why are you so angry with me?"

"I'm not." The denial came quickly.

"I thought we were friends, and all of a sudden you're treating me like I'm your worst enemy."

"I'm not mad."

"I haven't seen you in a week. Friends don't avoid each other like that."

"I've been busy." Even to his own ears, the excuse sounded lame.

"Friends are honest with each other," Lily continued, gesturing defensively.

"I haven't lied."

"Friends tell each other what's on their minds."

"Nothing's bothering me. Why can't you accept that?"

Lily made a tsking noise that sounded amazingly like Gram when she was displeased about something.

"All right," Jake countered in an angry huff. "You want to talk about friends? Fine. Then maybe you should think about what's been going on between us. You may be innocent, Lily Morrissey," Jake retorted, "but you're not naive enough to believe that friends kiss the way we do." Hoping to give the appearance of nonchalance, Jake leaned against the counter and crossed his arms. "I don't like what's happening."

"Nothing's happening," Lily said, struggling to keep her voice from rising. "We aren't any different than we were six months ago."

"The hell we aren't!"

"All right, I concede that our relationship has gone to a deeper level, but we're still good friends. At least that's what I'd like to think."

Jake snorted. "We're in serious trouble."

"You're being overdramatic. I...I like kissing you. You make me feel warm and tingly inside. I just don't think that's wrong."

"Not wrong; bad."

"You're saying that because you think kissing must mean something more."

Twin brows arched skeptically. "And it doesn't?"

"Not if we don't want it to."

"Lily." Her name came out in a rush of breath as if he were reasoning with a young child. "Kissing is only the first step. The next thing you know and we'll be in bed together and wondering how we ever managed to let things go so far."

"You seem to be equating a simple friendly kiss with love and marriage. Good grief, Jake. We're friends and we just happen to like to kiss each other. It isn't going to lead to anything.

"If we don't stop thinking like this, the next thing I know I'll be shopping for disposable diapers."

Unable to stop, Lily laughed. "Honestly, Jake, you make it sound far more dreadful than it is. Here, let me show you." She moved across the narrow confines of the cabin and placed her hands on his shoulders.

Jake stiffened and jerked away as if she'd burned him. "No."

"It's only a kiss, not a hand grenade."

"I don't want us kissing."

"But I want to prove something." Her voice was small and she couldn't keep the disappointment out of it. Now that they were clearing the air, Lily realized how much she had enjoyed the few kisses they'd shared. Before Jake had the opportunity to react, she tilted up her face and met his mouth in a soft caress.

Jake felt liquid fire seep through him. Even a light brush of her mouth over his was agony.

"See," Lily announced proudly. "And I'm not humming the 'Wedding March' or anything. From everything Gram's told me, there isn't the slightest possibility of my getting pregnant from a kiss."

What Jake was thinking didn't have anything to do with marriage and a family. His gaze fell past her to the small area where he slept. He thought about sleeping with Lily at his side and seeing her hair spread out on his pillow. The vision of her lying there without clothes and reaching her arms out to him nearly blinded him with a desire so deep that it ate a hole right through him.

"Right," he grumbled, having difficulty saying the lone word.

"To prove a point, I think we should do it again."

"I don't know." He closed his eyes, knowing that one pleading glance from Lily and he'd give her anything she wanted. He hated his lack of self-control. It had never been like this with any other woman. He had been the one in charge. Women came willingly to him. It wasn't supposed to be the other way around. He should be the strong and decisive one.

Jake opened his eyes to discover Lily standing so close that all he had to do was lean forward and their bodies would touch. He could feel the heat radiating from her. So little would be required of him to press his thigh to hers, to feel the rounded smoothness of her stomach to his abdomen or to have her full breasts nuzzle his chest. Oh Lord, his senses were awake to every delicate, womanly nuance of her and it was slowly driving him insane.

Unable to keep his hands away from her, Jake tenderly cupped her cheek. The thick dark lashes of her seductive eyes fluttered closed as she turned her face into his palm. Ever so gently with the lightest, briefest of caresses, she kissed the inside of his hand. Wild sensations swept up his arm. The inch or so between them was eliminated before another second had passed. They stood thigh to thigh, stomach to abdomen, breasts to chest, and feasted on the feel of each other. With a reverence that shocked him, Jake lowered his head and claimed Lily's mouth. Their lips clung in the sweetest, most profound kiss Lily had experienced in her life. Passion smoldered just beneath the surface, but this was a different kind of kiss—one that Lily didn't know how to define. Her hand crept up his chest and closed around the folds of his shirt collar as she clung to him.

When Jake lifted his mouth from hers, Lily smiled up at him and tears clouded her eyes. "That was beautiful," she whispered.

"You're beautiful." He tucked a strand of hair around her ear and caressed her temple with his fingertips.

"It's so good." She had that dreamy look of a woman in love.

Lightly, he kissed her again. "Lily, believe me when I tell you that this has to stop."

"Okay," she murmured. She looped her arms around his neck and buried her face in his throat. He smelled of the sea and the sun. Vital and alive. Her tongue discovered his pulse and she gloried in the wild fluttering movement.

"Lily," he groaned, moving his hands to set her away.

"You taste good."

Already it was happening. Against his will, he was giving in to her. He hadn't wanted her on his boat and here she was a few feet from his bed. He had argued with her about this kissing business and it had made no difference. They were in each other's arms, and from the way it was progressing, only heaven knew where they'd end up.

"I said, no more." Forcefully Jake moved away from her. He took two steps and abruptly turned around, going the identical distance in the opposite direction.

Shocked, Lily watched him, her expression a mixture of bewilderment and hurt.

"I told you before, I wanted to put an end to this nonsense. You women are all alike."

"Jake—"

"It was the same thing with Elaine." It hadn't been, but Lily didn't know that and Jake was desperate for a means of extracting himself before things went further. He had to act fast.

"I'm not anything like Elaine."

"That's the real problem. The two of you could be sisters. You think a woman has to drive a ring through a man's nose and lead him around."

"That's not true." Lily struggled to swallow back her indignation.

"Women are never satisfied. There's always something that needs to be changed."

"What have I ever asked you to change?"

"My writing. At first you were content to read the short stories, but oh no, those didn't make enough money, so you started pressing me to write novels."

"But I thought..."

"The crazy part of all this is that for a time I even considered it."

Lily took a step back, staring up at Jake. She slowly shook her head, still having trouble believing that it was Jake speaking to her—the man who only minutes ago had held her so lovingly in his arms and kissed her as though she were a priceless gift of porcelain.

"A woman can't stand the thought of a man being happy. She has to change him. Elaine nearly ruined my life and I almost let her. Thank God I saw the light in time."

"Jake..." Recklessly, Lily tried one last time to reason with him.

"You aren't any better than Elaine, worming your way into my life, using me, and then deciding to take it upon yourself to mold me into whatever it is you want."

"I've never tried to change you."

"Of course, that's the beauty of women. You want to save me. Well, listen and listen good. I like my life. I don't want to be saved. Got it?"

"Would you stop shouting long enough for me to say something?" Lily demanded, furious and struggling to show Jake that he wasn't making the least bit of sense.

"No. Enough's been said."

"It hasn't!" she shouted. "I like you the way you are and I have no intention of saving you."

Jake snorted. "That was what Elaine said."

"I'm not Elaine!" She stabbed a finger in his direction.

"Right," he snickered.

"There's no reasoning with you when you're like this."

"Then it would be best if you left, wouldn't it?"

Tears glistened like diamonds in her eyes and her body trembled with the effort to restrain their fall. "In other words, you're asking me to leave?"

"I'm saying—"

"Don't say anything . . . it's not necessary. I get the picture." Dropping her head, she nervously rubbed her palms together in a slow movement meant to disguise her distress. "I won't bother you again . . . and I'll never, ever come on board the *Lucky Lady* again. You've made your point perfectly clear." She turned quickly and moved up the steps with an agility born of emotional pain and shock.

Jake didn't move. Above him, he heard Lily's footsteps as she hurried across the deck. Her steps were heavy and their echoing sound cut straight into Jake's heart. The frustrations of a lifetime of disillusionment and bitterness suddenly surfaced and he struggled against the urge to ram his fist through the side of the boat. He paced the tiny, enclosed area in an effort to compose himself. It was what he wanted. Lily was gone. He didn't doubt her word; she wouldn't be back. He'd driven her away by attacking her motives and her pride.

But Jake couldn't imagine what his life would be like without her. There were better ways of handling this situation. He could apologize, but doubted the wisdom of it. No, he'd bide his time and try to forget how hard it was to let her go. That was the only solution to avoid ruining both their lives.

By the time Lily slid onto the mahogany bench at the grand piano in the Wheaton's huge lobby that evening, she was outwardly composed. But the inner battle continued to rage. She didn't know which had hurt the most—Jake comparing her to that horrible Elaine, or when he'd told her to leave his boat. Both had devastated her to the point that she hadn't been able to talk to Gram. Once she'd arrived home, Lily had gone directly to her room and sat staring into space. When the tears came, she moved into the bathroom and stepped into the shower, allowing the water to conceal her pain. A cold washcloth over her eyes had eventually brought her face from the fiery red of tears to a healthy, if not misleading, pink.

Lily placed her hands over the ivory piano keys and the fingers responded automatically, playing of their own accord. Lily had learned not to involve her mind in the music. If she did, she'd have been half-crazy by now. Her smile was pasted on her mouth, curving her full lips slightly upward.

The manager strolled past her once and Lily dropped her gaze to her hands. Usually his presence meant she had done something that annoyed him. Lily no longer cared. If he fired her, she'd find another job. The monotony of playing the same songs night after night had robbed her musical gift of the natural spark she'd once possessed. She hardly ever sat at the piano to goof around anymore. And all this for what. The only wealthy man she'd met in a year's time at the hotel was Rex Flanders and that had turned out to be a bust. Even now, Jake's negative reaction to the Texan surprised her. He hadn't so much as seen Rex and he'd forced Lily into promising that she wouldn't go out with the middle-aged man.

When Lily had finished the first half of the evening's set of music, she took a break. Henry, the senior bellhop, stopped her halfway across the lobby.

"Miss Lily, there's a message for you." He strolled across the carpet to hand her a beige envelope.

Lily accepted the letter and her heart gave a tiny flip-flop reaction. For one insane moment, Lily thought it might be from Jake. After a glance at the slanted strokes of the cursive script, she recognized the handwriting as Rex Flanders's.

The first genuine smile of the evening touched her tired eyes. The moment she had time to herself, Lily carefully tore open the envelope.

Hello Lily,
I've been thinking about you lately, and about that old song you hunted up for me. As I promised, I'm back in San Francisco and I'm hoping that you'll allow me to show you my appreciation. I meant what I said about taking you to dinner. I insist. It's the least I can do to thank you.
I'll meet you in the lobby at nine-thirty. Don't disappoint me this time.

Rex

Folding the single sheet over, Lily tucked it inside the envelope. She would join Rex for dinner. Her promise to Jake had been made under duress. Besides, Jake meant nothing to her or Gram anymore.

He'd made his views plain. He had no reason to care if she saw Rex or any other man, for that matter.

Parked outside the Wheaton, Jake leaned against the side of his cab and crossed his arms, watching the entrance. Lily was due out in another hour. He needed to talk to her and explain that he hadn't meant what he'd said. The anger had been a ploy to keep her out of his arms, but he hadn't meant to insult her. An apology burned in his chest. The minute she came out of the Wheaton he would go to her and admit he was wrong. That was the very least he could do. She deserved that and a lot more.

Once he'd made his peace with Lily, Jake decided, they had to have a serious discussion about what was going on between them. They had to stop pretending their kisses didn't mean something, that they were simply friends. For his part, Jake was convinced that a serious relationship between them wouldn't work. Their goals couldn't be any more different. He wasn't going to change. And if Lily wanted a wealthy man, then he'd advise her to look elsewhere. She was putting her schemes in jeopardy by flirting with him.

They were reasonable adults. After they had talked this craziness out of their systems, they could go back to the way things used to be, and continue as friends. They had to acknowledge those feelings for what they were—infatuation. He was flattered that Lily found him attractive. But it could be only one or the other. They could be great friends or they could be good lovers. Of the two, Jake sought her friendship.

Satisfied with his reasoning, Jake checked his watch once again. She'd be out in another forty minutes, and they could talk then. A crooked grin slanted his mouth. He felt one hell of a lot better now than he had this afternoon.

Nervously, Lily smoothed a wrinkle from the chiffon skirt of her blue dress. She glanced up to find Rex strolling toward her, his eyes alight with appreciation.

"Lily," he whispered, and collected her hands. "You're as lovely as I remember."

Lily's long lashes fluttered downward. Rex looked even bigger and taller than she had recalled. "Thank you."

"Have you been waiting long?"

"No. Only a minute." Actually, she'd changed her mind twice. Not until she had got to the huge glass doors at the Wheaton's entrance had she decided to go back and meet Rex.

"Good." His gaze claimed hers. "It doesn't seem a whole month since I first laid eyes on you."

"Time has a way of slipping past, doesn't it?" Once she'd worried about appearing witty and attractive. Now she didn't care; she could only be herself.

"It sure does." He offered her his elbow in gentlemanly fashion. "I know a quiet little French restaurant where the food is excellent."

"That sounds lovely."

"You do like French food?"

"Oh, yes."

Smiling at her, Rex directed Lily toward the front entrance. Once outside, he stepped forward and raised his hand, calling for a taxi.

Jake was parked in the driveway, chewing on the end of a toothpick, wondering what was taking Lily so long. He had almost made up his mind to go inside and find out. As he straightened, the toothpick slipped unheeded from his mouth and fell to the ground. Lily was with that Texan. Jake was incredulous. She'd only mentioned the man a couple of times, but Jake knew instantly that he was the one escorting Lily. She'd promised not to see that pot-bellied fool again. Promised. Hell, he had been right. She wasn't any different from Elaine.

Too stupefied to react quickly, Jake watched as one of his colleagues pulled toward the front. The doorman opened the cab door and Lily climbed in the back with the Texan. Jake was so furious that he slammed his fist against the side of his taxi, momentarily paralyzing his fingers.

Well, fine, Lily could do whatever she liked. She was nothing to him. Nothing.

Inside the cab, Lily turned and tossed a look over her shoulder, wondering if Jake had been out front. Silently she cursed herself for being so utterly optimistic to even look. He wouldn't be there, of course. Why tonight, after a whole week of avoiding her? After what had happened that afternoon, the Wheaton would be the last place Jake would show.

Agitatedly, Lily fiddled with her fingers. She regretted having agreed to go with Rex. It had been a childish thing to do, and she'd accepted the date for all the wrong reasons.

Rex must have sensed her uneasiness since he chatted the whole way, his deep voice filling the taxi. When she responded with only a polite word or two, he struck up a conversation with the cab driver.

Lily wondered if the driver, who was a friend of Jake's, would mention it to him. Fervently she prayed he wouldn't, then doubted that Jake would care either way.

The restaurant, Chez Philippe, was one of the most expensive and highly rated in all San Francisco. Famous people from all over the world were reputed to have dined there. Lily had often dreamed of sampling the excellent cuisine and catching a glimpse of a movie star.

After arriving at the restaurant, they were seated by the maitre d' and handed huge, odd-shaped menus. Lily noted that hers didn't list the prices, so she was left to guess at what this dinner would cost Rex. However, she learned long ago that anyone who needed to ask prices probably couldn't afford it.

"Do you see anything that looks good to you, little filly?"

Their eyes met over the top of the menu. "What would you suggest?" Gram had taught her to ask such a question when she was uncertain. The ploy wouldn't work this time and she doubted that Rex would be concerned with anything as minor as the cost of a meal.

Rex listed a couple of items and Lily smiled absently. The waiter returned and filled their water glasses with expensive bottled water.

With each passing minute, Jake's anger grew until he could almost taste his fury with every breath. Slamming the door of his cab, he cursed his lack of decisive action when he'd seen Lily with the rich Texan. She'd promised him she wouldn't see Daddy Warbucks again and with God as his witness, Jake was going to hold her to her word. As hard as it was on his patience, he waited until the cabbie who drove Lily and the Texan returned to the Wheaton.

"Where'd you take them?" Jake demanded in a tone that caused the other driver to cringe.

"Who?"

"You know who. Lily."

"Oh, yeah. That was her, wasn't it?"

Jake had never been able to abide this joker, and wouldn't need much of an excuse to ram his teeth down his throat. He grabbed the other man by the collar and half lifted him out of the car window.

The other driver turned unnaturally pale. "Jake, buddy, I didn't know. Hell, what was I supposed to do? Turn down a fare because you got a thing for this girl? Be reasonable, will ya?"

"Where did you take them?" Jake demanded a second time, relaxing his grip on the other man's collar.

The driver cleared his throat. "That fancy French place on Thirty-third."

"Chez Philippe's?"

"Right."

Jake released him and the other man ran a hand over his throat. "No need getting so hot. I was only doing my job."

Jake didn't bother to respond. He strode back to his cab and revved the engine with such force that a billow of black smoke shot from the tailpipe.

With an urgency that drove him to the point of recklessness, Jake roared through the streets. He ran two yellow lights and prayed a cop wouldn't pick him up along the way.

Once he was within a block of the restaurant, Jake pulled to a dead stop. What was he going to do once he arrived? To rush in and demand that Lily leave with him simply wouldn't work. He'd only end up looking like an idiot. He could picture her now, looking up at him with shock and disdain and quietly asking him to leave. No, he had to use more finesse than to rush in there.

He parked on the street because he didn't want the valet to take his cab. The fact was, Jake wasn't sure the valet *would* take it.

Hands buried deep inside his pants pockets, Jake strolled into the classy place as if he'd been dining there for years. The maitre d' stepped forward expectantly.

"May I help you, *monsieur*?"

"A table for one." Jake admired the guy for not saying a word. Obviously Jake wasn't dressed for a place like this.

"*Monsieur*, I regret that we only seat gentlemen wearing a suit and tie."

"You mean I have to have a suit and tie even before I can spend my money?"

"That is correct. I sincerely regret the inconvenience."

Jake scowled. "Do you mind if I sit and wait?" He motioned toward an empty chair.

"Sir, we aren't going to change our dress code this evening."

"That's fine, I'd just like to wait."

The stoic expression altered for the first time as the maitre d' arched a skeptical brow. "As you wish."

The low whispers in the front of the restaurant caused Lily to glance up from her plate. As she did, her breath caught in her lungs. Jake was standing there, and from the look he tossed at her, he was furious.

Their eyes clashed and his narrowed with such malice that Lily immediately lowered hers.

Chapter Eight

Lily felt the blood drain from her face and her stomach do a minisomersault. Jake was in the restaurant, looking at her as if it required every ounce of good taste he'd ever possessed not to march across the room and jerk her out of her chair.

"Doesn't that sound like fun?" Rex was saying.

Lily stared at him blankly. The fact he'd spoken had barely registered in her numbed state. "Yes, it does." She hoped her response was appropriate.

"Good. Good," Rex continued, obviously pleased. "I thought a young filly like you would enjoy an evening on the town."

The first time she'd met Rex, Lily had torn Gram's house apart looking for that crazy song on the chance he'd suggest spending an evening with her. A lavish date with a rich man had been Lily's dream for many years. She was a fool if she was going to allow Jake's foul temper to ruin tonight. With a small display of pride, she forced her chin up a notch. Jake had made his views of her plain, and she wasn't going to let him wreck her evening.

"I'd love to do the town. Where would you like to start?" She planted her elbows on top of the white linen tablecloth and propped her face in her hands so that they framed her pale cheeks. She fluttered her long lashes at Rex in a way she knew would call attention to the dark depth of her eyes.

"There's a small dance floor at the St. Francis."

"That sounds grand," Lily simpered.

"We could have our after-dinner drink there as well, if you like."

"That would be fine."

From the corner of her eye, Lily noted that Jake was pacing the small area in front of the maitre d's desk. A tiny smile tugged at the edges of her mouth. She hoped he got an eyeful. The memory of the many insults he'd hurled at her earlier was enough to encourage Lily. She wasn't much of a flirt; she didn't know how. But with Rex sitting across from her and Jake just waiting for the opportunity to pounce on her, Lily gave the act all she had.

Jake had claimed she was a schemer; she was only proving him right. Once he saw the way she behaved with Rex, he would get the message and leave.

The waiter approached their table with the bill. While Rex dealt with it, Lily took the opportunity to glance in Jake's direction. The shock of seeing him had faded and was developing into righteous anger. As far as Lily was concerned, Jake had one hell of a nerve to even come near her.

"Are you ready?" Rex asked.

"Yes." Despite her indignation and steely resolve, Lily's heart constricted as Rex pulled out her chair and she stood.

Her wealthy escort placed a hand in the small of her back, urging her forward. Lily looked up at him with adoring eyes, ignoring Jake. She held her breath as they approached the front desk, wondering if he would cause a scene. Indecision showed in his brilliant green eyes and she quickly glanced away.

For his part, Jake battled with uncertainty. He'd been a fool to have followed her there. By all that felt right, he should punch out the lights of that oil-rich Texan and grab Lily while he had the chance. But he couldn't do that. Lily would never forgive him and he already owed her one apology.

The chiffon hem of her skirt brushed his leg as she scooted past him and Jake jumped back as though he'd been burned. His eyes demanded that she look at him, but Lily refused to shift her gaze from her sugar daddy. She tucked her hand in the crook of the Texan's elbow and glanced up at him with a look that reminded Jake of melted honey.

Unsure of what he should do, Jake stood as he was for an entire minute, silently cursing. If he had any sense left, which he was sincerely beginning to doubt, he'd go back to the marina and forget that Lily had broken her promise.

Once outside, Jake's feet felt as though they were weighted with concrete blocks as he walked down the small flight of stairs. He touched his forehead in a companionable salute as he passed the valet.

Lily and the Texan were in the back seat of another cab, pulling out of the circular driveway and Jake stepped back as they sped away.

As Jake returned to his taxi his footsteps increased their pace. He couldn't ignore the gut feeling that something was wrong with Lily and Rex. The *feeling* had always perplexed him. He hadn't *felt* right about Lily and Rick either, but this time the sensation was far stronger. If anything happened to Lily, he'd never be able to forgive himself. Foolish pride no longer dictated his actions; he was driven by something far stronger: fear.

His hand slapped the side of the taxi and he jumped inside and revved the engine. It only took a minute to locate the other cab driving Lily and Rex. Jake stayed a fair distance behind them, fearing that the other driver would suspect that he was following him and mention it to Lily and company.

When they entered the downtown area, Jake relaxed. The second cab was in his territory now and Jake wove in and out of traffic without a problem. The driver dropped Lily and the Texan off at the St. Francis Hotel and Jake cocked his head slightly. He couldn't fault the man's taste. Jake rounded the corner and was lucky enough to locate a parking space.

The doorman opened the huge glass door as Jake approached the hotel entrance. Music from the piano bar filtered into the lobby area from the cocktail lounge and he sauntered in there. Although his gait was casual, his eyes carefully scanned the darkened area for Lily. When he spotted her sitting at a tiny table in the middle of the room, he heaved a sigh of relief.

As inconspicuously as possible, he took a seat at the far corner of the bar so he could keep an eye on her without her suspecting that he was there.

"Can I help you?" The bartender spoke and Jake swiveled his attention from Lily to him.

"Give me a beer."

"Right away."

Sitting sideways, Jake propped an elbow against the edge of the bar and centered his attention on Lily. The old familiar sensations stirred within him. She really was lovely. Jake couldn't blame Rex for finding Lily attractive. Jake recalled the day he'd taken her out on the *Lucky Lady* and the way she'd sat on the bow, laughing. The wind had tossed her hair in every direction and she had resembled a sea nymph, sitting there soaking in the early summer sun. Something had happened to him that day—something so significant that he had yet to determine its true meaning. From that moment on, Jake concluded, his life had been in a tailspin.

The bartender delivered his beer and Jake absently placed a bill on the counter. Holding the thick glass with one hand, he took a deep swallow of the brew. It felt cool and soothing against his parched throat. He set the glass back on the bar.

Glancing in Lily's direction again, Jake noted that Rex had reached for her hand and held it in his own and was leaning across the small table, talking intimately with her. From this distance Jake couldn't read Lily's reaction.

Without being aware of it, Jake slid off the bar stool and braced his feet. His fist knotted and with gut-wrenching resolve he managed to control his immediate outrage. Another man was touching Lily and although it appeared innocent enough, Jake didn't like it. He didn't like it one damn bit. Furthermore, he trusted that overweight Texan about as much as he did a rattlesnake.

Several couples were dancing in a small area on the other side of the cocktail lounge and Jake watched as Rex stood and brought Lily to her feet. Jake downed the remainder of his beer when the Texan escorted Lily to the dance floor and brought her into the circle of his arms. Holding hands was one thing, but dancing was another. There was nothing more Jake could do, he resolved, but act. He ate up the distance to the dance floor in three huge strides.

Lily wished she hadn't agreed to come to the bar with Rex. Nothing was going right and she felt like a fraud. She had no desire to share a drink and conversation and had even less enthusiasm for dancing. Rex's hands felt warm and clammy against her back and she resisted the subtle pressure of his arms to press her closer.

They'd swayed around the small dance area once when Lily glanced up and noticed Jake coming toward her with abrupt, angry strides. She knew she should be furious, but her heart responded with a wild leap of pleasure. After her act in the restaurant, Lily had been sick with self-disgust. Rex was a nice man. He didn't deserve to be used as a ploy to rile Jake. As guilty as she'd felt, Lily had had trouble maintaining a decent conversation with Rex. She could only guess what Rex thought of her. Probably the worst, and she couldn't blame him.

Jake wedged himself between two dancing couples to tap Rex's shoulder. "I'm cutting in." He didn't ask, but simply announced it.

Rex looked stunned. "Lily?"

"That's fine," she murmured, dropping her gaze. "I...I know him. This is Jake Carson."

Jake took Lily by the waist, pressing her to him as he whirled her away.

"Jake—"

"No, you listen to me. What kind of game are you playing?" He pushed the words through clenched teeth. He was furious and unreasonable and didn't care. After the chase she'd put him through tonight he wanted answers.

"I'm not playing..."

"You assured me that you wouldn't be seeing Daddy Warbucks."

"That was before."

"Before what?"

"Before you *assured me* that I was a nuisance and asked me to leave your precious boat."

"Consequently your promise doesn't mean anything?"

"No," she cried, then changed her mind. "Yes."

"Dinner was bad enough, but did you have to drag him here as well? What's the matter? Didn't that fancy restaurant give you ample opportunity to flaunt yourself?"

Lily was too outraged to answer him. "Let me go."

"No. I'm taking you home."

"Rex can escort me to Gram's."

"No way. You told me you wouldn't be seeing that rich bullfrog, and I'm holding you to your word."

"You can't make me do anything." Lily couldn't understand why she was fighting Jake when she was so glad he was there. If he would stop behaving like an arrogant fool, she'd tell him that she longed for him to take her home.

"I don't have much taste for a scene, but I won't back away from one if that's what you want. But be warned: I don't need an excuse to ram Rex's teeth down his silver-plated throat."

"You're nothing more than a bully."

"Perhaps."

"There's no question about it. You're bossy, stubborn and unreasonable."

"Great. Now that you've named my personality traits we can leave."

"Not without saying something to Rex."

Jake relaxed his hold. "I'll do the talking."

"That's hardly necessary."

He didn't answer and instead gripped her hand in his and led the way off the dance floor. The other couples cleared a path for them and Lily wondered how much of their heated conversation had been heard by the other dancers. Embarrassment brought a heated flash of bright color to her cheeks.

Rex stood as they approached the small table.

"I'm taking Lily home," Jake informed the older man without preamble.

"Lily?" Rex eyed her seriously. His brows formed into a sharp frown as he waited for her to respond.

The pressure Jake applied to her hand was nearly crippling, but Lily was convinced he had no idea he was hurting her.

"Jake's an old friend," she said, trying to explain.

"I see," Rex said slowly.

"I hope you do," Jake added. His hand continued to grip hers as he headed out of the cocktail lounge, half pulling Lily as he went.

In her high heels she had difficulty keeping up with his wide strides and paused momentarily to toss an apologetic look over her shoulder, wanting Rex to know she was sorry for everything.

"Are you happy?" she asked, once they hit the sidewalk.

"Very." He thrust his face toward her. "Don't ever pull that trick on me again."

With every ounce of the ladylike behavior Gram had drilled into her over the years, Lily battled to keep her temper. She only partially succeeded. "And don't you *ever* do that to me again."

"Keep your promises and I won't," Jake barked.

They didn't say another word until they were inside the cab and on the street.

The anger was slowly dissolving inside Lily. Everything had changed in the past few weeks and she didn't know if it was for the better. A year ago, she'd started playing piano at the Wheaton with so many expectations. In that time she'd dated two wealthy men and met Jake. Rick and Rex weren't anything like she'd dreamed. Jake was Jake: proud, stubborn, pigheaded and very good to her and Gram. She'd experienced a gnawing ache over the loss of something precious and wonderful—her relationship with Jake—and prayed it wasn't too late to salvage it.

"I thought you didn't care anymore what I did," she murmured, longing to explain why she'd accepted Rex's invitation.

"Believe me, it wasn't by choice." His hand compressed around the steering wheel, pressing grooved indentations into his fingers.

"Then why did you . . ."

"I could care less who you see," he lied smoothly. "But you'd given your word and I was determined to see that you kept it."

"That's why you followed me tonight?" Her voice was little more than a husky whisper.

"Right."

"I see," she mumbled and clasped her hands together tightly in her lap. She'd hoped that he'd admit that he cared for her and had been concerned about her welfare. But that was clearly too much to expect in his present frame of mind.

Jake dropped her off in front of Gram's and drove away as soon as she closed the car door. She didn't chance looking at him. His features, sharpened by anger, were so achingly familiar that Lily couldn't have borne seeing his displeasure another time.

Once inside the house she struggled to keep a grip on her composure. Gram was asleep and Lily was grateful. She would have had trouble recounting the events of this evening. Nothing had gone right, starting with accepting Rex's invitation to dinner.

Knowing that any effort to sleep would be useless, Lily wandered into the kitchen. In the blur of bitter tears, she set water on the burner to boil. When the kettle whistled, she poured the boiling liquid into the instant coffee and cupped the mug with both hands, absorbing its burning heat.

A loud knock against the front door surprised her and her heart rocketed to her throat. She didn't have time to react when Jake burst in.

"We need to talk," he announced, coming toward her.

Lily couldn't have moved if her life depended on it.

"Well?" he demanded.

"Would you like a cup of coffee?" Lily noticed that his defenses relaxed at the offer.

"Yes."

She busied herself bringing down another cup from the cupboard and dissolving the dark crystals in the steaming water. The action gave her precious moments to compose her thoughts. Her head filled with all the things she longed to say. As much as she tried, she couldn't keep her gaze off the man who filled the doorway. Jake stood motionless, staring at her.

"Would you like to sit down?" she offered, gesturing toward the chair. Lily found it short of amazing that only minutes before they had been shouting at each other and now they were behaving like polite strangers.

She set the second steaming mug across from her own on the tabletop and took a chair. For lack of something better to occupy her hands, she gripped the mug and stared into the black liquid.

The silence grew heavy and Lily was unsure if she should be the first one to wade into it.

"Lily—"

"Jake—"

They spoke simultaneously. "You first," Jake said and motioned toward her with his hand.

"No . . . you go first."

"All right." Another lengthy pause followed. "I'm here to apologize."

"For what?"

"Come on, Lily, don't play dumb." Challenge glinted from his steady gaze.

"I'm not." Her own temper fired anew. "Are you apologizing for this afternoon or tonight."

Jake raked his fingers through his hair and Lily watched him covertly. The kitchen suddenly felt small and Jake seemed so large, filling every corner. Even the nerves in her body were conscious of him. She longed to feel his arms around her again, comforting and gentle.

"I see," Jake said finally. "I guess I do owe you an apology for both." His finger fiddled with the rim of the mug. As yet he hadn't tasted the coffee, but then neither had Lily.

"I owe you one myself. I don't know what craziness possessed me to accept Rex Flanders's dinner invitation. I should never have gone. I don't even know why I did." Her voice kept getting huskier. "That's not exactly true. I went with him because I wanted to get back at you for this afternoon."

"I didn't mean what I said." A telltale muscle twitched along his jaw.

Lily raised her eyes to Jake's, unsure that she had understood him correctly.

"Those things I said on the boat were spoken in desperation."

"But why?"

"Come on, Lily, surely you've figured it out by now." He pushed back the chair and stood, taking his coffee with him as he marched to the sink and then turned back to her. He leaned against the counter and tasted his coffee.

"You mean because we were kissing again?"

"Bingo."

"But I like kissing you."

"That's the problem, kid."

Lily winced at the use of the childish term. "Why didn't you say so? We don't ever have to touch each other again."

It wasn't what Jake wanted, but for his peace of mind and for the sake of a treasured relationship, he had little choice but to claim exactly that. "That would be best."

"The kissing was just the result of my own curiosity."

"So you said."

Lily's heart was hammering in her throat. She was forced to admit how much she'd come to enjoy Jake's touch and the thought of them never kissing again produced a heavy sadness within her. Purposely she took a sip of the coffee, which had grown lukewarm.

Jake followed suit. There didn't seem to be anything more to say but he didn't want to leave, so he searched for an excuse to linger. "You were right about me being a unreasonable bully this evening."

"I don't blame you." She released a short, audible breath that told of her own regrets. "That was such a childish thing to do I can't believe I'd stoop to anything so low."

"So you knew I was waiting tonight."

"No." Her gaze found his. She'd hoped, of course, but she hadn't guessed that he'd be there after their confrontation on the sailboat. "My feelings were hurt and I didn't think you'd care one way or the other if I saw Rex—especially after today—so I agreed to the dinner. I regretted it almost from the minute we left the hotel."

"You seemed to be enjoying your meal." His jaw clenched at the memory of Lily in that fancy French restaurant.

Lily swallowed at the lump of pride that constricted her throat. She'd come this far. "That was an act for your benefit."

"What?" Jake exploded.

"I was mad!"

"So you wanted to make me suffer."

"It's stupid, I know, but at the time it made sense."

A crooked grin lifted one corner of his mouth. "You're lucky that making a scene in that restaurant didn't make sense—at the time."

"I guess I am at that." She returned his smile, wondering if there would ever be a time when his laughing eyes wouldn't affect her.

Jake made a show of glancing at his watch. "I suppose I should think about heading home." A few more nights like this one and he'd have trouble paying his bills.

"It is late." Lily couldn't disagree with that, but she didn't want him to leave. She never did.

He took one last swallow of the coffee and placed the mug in the sink. "I'm pleased that we were able to resolve our differences."

"We were both wrong."

"Are you working tomorrow?" He already knew she wasn't, but asking delayed his departure.

"No."

"How about an afternoon on the boat?" The invitation was the least he could do after making such an issue of her leaving.

Instantly her dark eyes brightened. Lily loved the *Lucky Lady*, and the thought of spending a carefree afternoon with Jake was an opportunity she wouldn't refuse. "You're sure?"

No, he wasn't. The day would probably end up being nothing but pure torture for him. Having Lily at his side all afternoon and being forced to pretend he didn't notice how enticing she was could not be termed enjoyable.

"Jake?"

"I invited you, didn't I?"

"Then I'd love it."

"It's a date then. Can you meet me around noon?"

"I'll be there." She followed him through the living room to the front door. "Jake."

He turned, his brow knit with a heavy frown. Already he wished he hadn't issued the sailing invitation. His thoughtless words from earlier in the day demanded some form of retribution. "Yeah?"

"Thank you for coming back. I wouldn't have been able to sleep if you hadn't."

His harsh features relaxed. "Me either." With that he was gone.

The following morning Lily was humming as she worked around the kitchen. She had a lemon meringue pie baking in the oven and was whipping together pastrami sandwiches when Gram returned from the garden nursery. The older woman carted in an armload of potted plants.

At Lily's dubious look, Gram explained, "They were on sale."

Continuing to pack the sandwiches, Lily commented, "But aren't you the one who insists that we don't save money by spending money?"

"Good grief, no."

"Are you sure?" Lily tried unsuccessfully to hide a smile.

"Of course I'm sure. I may be seventy-four, but my mind is still good. I'm the one who says that when the going gets tough, the tough go shopping."

Despite her efforts not to, Lily burst into happy peals of laughter. "I love you, Gram. I don't think I let you know that nearly often enough."

"Sure you do, girl."

Impulsively, Lily hugged her grandmother. Gram might be a bit eccentric, but she had given Lily a good life, taking her in and raising her with a heartful of love. "I've got some news for you."

"What?" Gram leafed through the mail, tossing half of it away without so much as opening it. The rest she stuffed into an overflowing vase on the tabletop.

"I'm giving the Wheaton my two-week notice."

A worried frown narrowed the wrinkled brow. "Now why do that?"

"I don't like it there. This morning I called a day-care center and made an appointment to see the director. The ad in the paper said they were looking for a music director."

"And you'd like that?" Gram regarded her skeptically.

"I'm sure I would. You know how much I like children."

"That you do. You're as natural with them as you are with us old folks."

Opening the refrigerator, Lily scouted its contents, taking out two red apples.

"You going somewhere?"

"Jake and I are taking out the *Lucky Lady*."

Gram sank into the kitchen chair and lifted her feet to the opposite chair. "Rick phoned last night. I forgot to tell you."

"What did he want?"

"Just to remind you that he was taking you to dinner tonight."

Lily bit into her bottom lip. "Darn." She'd forgotten about that. "Did he say what time he'd be by?"

"Seven. He didn't seem too happy when I told him you were going out with that fellow from Texas."

Hands on her hips, Lily swiveled around. She'd phoned Gram during her break to explain why she'd be late. "You told him?"

"Had to, girl. He was planning on picking you up after work."

"Great," Lily mumbled sarcastically. On second thought it was probably just as well. Rick had been getting far too serious lately; he'd made several leading comments that had troubled her. But Rick was nice and deserved someone who would appreciate him.

"How well do you like this Rick fellow?" Gram wanted to know.

"He's all right."

"Seems to be well off."

"He's got money, if that's what you mean."

"That's what you've been wanting."

The words had a brittle edge to them. Lily opened her mouth to argue that Gram made her sound calculating and shallow, but she found she had no argument. That was exactly the way she'd been thinking lately. Her ambition to marry rich had made her so narrow-minded that it was little wonder she'd been disappointed with both Rick and Rex.

"I'm not so sure anymore," Lily murmured, tucking the lunch supplies into the bottom of a wicker basket. "I've been doing some thinking lately and I feel that there are certain things in life more valuable than a fat checkbook."

"Oh?" Gram gave her a look of mock surprise.

"Money's nice, but it isn't everything."

"The next time house taxes are due I'll tell that to the county clerk."

"We've always managed in the past; we'll do so again."

Gram mumbled something under her breath, but she was smiling and Lily wondered what her game was.

"So you're going to spend the day with Jake. I take it you two have resolved your differences."

"You could say that," Lily hedged. They'd taken one step forward, but at the moment it seemed a small one. There was so much she wanted to share with Jake and feared she couldn't. Her job at the Wheaton was coming to an end, but she wouldn't tell Jake until she had another job to replace it. Otherwise he'd fret. He cared for Gram and her. Lily only wished he cared a little bit more.

Chapter Nine

Jake placed the jib sail on the bow of the *Lucky Lady*. He wasn't looking forward to this excursion with Lily and regretted having suggested it. However, he realized that Lily loved being on the water and that the invitation to sail was his means of apologizing. He'd behaved like a fool over that rich Texan and Lily deserved some form of compensation for his actions.

Strolling down the long narrow dock that led to Jake's boat, Lily saw him working on the bow. She paused and felt a warmth surround her heart at the sight of the lean, brawny figure he made. He was all male, rugged and so completely different from Rick that it was difficult to picture them as friends. Jake possessed an indomitable spirit and a fierce pride. Of the two men, Rick was the more urbane and sophisticated. Jake's features were too strong to be considered suave. But there was a purity of character in Jake. He would have scoffed if Lily had ever thought to mention it. But the fact remained. Rick was too easily influenced by those around him. He considered it important to flow with the tide. Jake was the type of man who *moved* the tide.

"Morning," she called, standing on the pier and waving at him.

"Good morning." Jake straightened and Lily noted the faint grimness to his mouth. He wasn't pleased to be sailing today. He was doing this for her.

Revealing some enthusiasm, she held up the picnic basket. "I packed us a lunch."

"Good thinking." He climbed down from the bow, granting her a glimpse of his firmly muscled stomach beneath the front of his unbuttoned shirt. "Are you ready to cast off?"

"Aye, aye, captain." She gave him a mock salute and handed him the basket before climbing aboard. While he fiddled with the ropes, Lily took off her light summer jacket. She'd worn jeans and a sleeveless top, hoping to catch a bit of a tan on her pale arms. She didn't hold out much hope for this day, but desperately yearned to smooth over the rough edges of their relationship. Jake had been such a good friend. There were things in her life that only Jake knew. She could tell him anything without fear of being criticized or harshly judged. Anyone else would have called her hard-hearted and callous to set her sights on a wealthy man. Not Jake. He'd even gone so far as to introduce her to Rick and to try to help her fulfill her ambitions. And she had helped him. Jake longed to be a writer. He could do it, too. The *New Yorker* wouldn't buy a short story from someone without talent.

"We're going to have nice weather," Jake said, looking to the blue sky.

"Yes, we are." They were tiptoeing around each other, Lily realized, each afraid of the other's response. They feared doing or saying something that would offend the other. "Can I raise the sails again?"

"If you want." He kept his sights straight ahead, manning the helm.

Feeling self-conscious and a little unsteady on her feet, Lily climbed to the bow, prepared to raise the sails. She waited until they were clear of the waterway that led from the marina to the deep, greenish waters of San Francisco Bay before hoisting the sails and tying them off. The boat instantly keeled and sliced through the rolling waves.

Holding on to the mast, Lily threw back her head and raised her closed eyes to the warm rays of the summer sun. A sense of exhilaration and power filled her. Her unbound hair blew behind her head like a flag waving in the breeze. She loved this. Her skin tingled with the force of the wind and the spray of saltwater. Nothing mattered when she could savor these exquisite moments of freedom.

"This is great," she called down to Jake a moment later. Finding a comfortable spot, she sat and wrapped her arms around her bent knees, soaking up the other sensations as much as the warm sun. She felt marvelous—better than she had in weeks. She was giddy with happiness and feeling a bit reckless, but not so rash as to tempt fate by sitting near Jake. She looked at him and their eyes met. Lily's cheeks grew warm as he studied her. His eyes became serious and narrowed, and seemed to linger on her mouth. Tremulously she smiled at him. He responded with a short, almost involuntary, grin.

Jake's eyes feasted on Lily. He seemed incapable of looking away. She was so lovely that the picture of her at this moment, her dark hair wind-tossed and free, would be forever seared in his mind. Her mouth was so soft and luscious that he yearned to go to her, kneel at her feet, and lay his life before her.

His heart slammed painfully against his chest and he felt as if an invisible fist had punched him in the abdomen. He was in love with Lily. The emotion he felt for her went far beyond friendship. He was in love with her the way a man loves a woman. He found his own stupidity unbelievable. All these weeks he'd been in love with her and hadn't admitted it—not even to himself. The thought crashed into his mind with such force that Jake stopped breathing. All right, he reasoned, he loved her. He'd always loved her. Now what? A frown drove deep grooves in his brow. Nothing. He'd always cared for her. Recognizing his feelings couldn't make a difference. Lily was as sweet and innocent as a fresh morning rose. She wanted material possessions that he could never give her. She was meant for minks and expensive perfume. From the pittance he earned driving a taxi and writing stories, it was unlikely that he could ever afford either. He might love her, but he wouldn't use that love to destroy her dreams.

From her position aft, Lily studied Jake, wanting to memorize everything about him. His eyes had always fascinated her as had his face with the hard angles and sandpaper cheeks with the five o'clock shadow. His look now was intense, dark. She couldn't recall a time when he'd been more withdrawn.

Concerned, she cupped her hands around her mouth and called forward: "Are you hungry?"

For a moment Jake stared into the sunshine, not answering. "I could eat something." Actually, he was ravenous but he feared problems once Lily joined him on deck. Now that he'd acknowledged his feelings, it would be ten times more difficult to keep her out of his arms.

Lily hadn't eaten since early morning. "I'm starving." Watching her step, she worked her way toward the front of the boat and joined him a minute later.

Jake watched her movements with lazy appraisal. The sun glittered through her hair, giving it an almost heavenly shine. Her lips were pink and so inviting that the muscles in his abdomen tightened. She moved with an unconscious grace. Each step she took emphasized the lovely lines of her neck and shoulders and the intriguing uplift of her breasts ... Jake's thoughts came to an abrupt halt. This type of thinking wouldn't do either of them good. He could fantasize until doomsday about making love to Lily and it wouldn't change anything. She was going to marry some rich man and Jake was going to let her.

Lily glanced up from the picnic basket to find Jake watching her with a look that was a mixture of anger and amusement. "Is something funny?"

"No." His gaze shot past her and on to the water, but when he turned back to her he smiled, his face relaxing and his eyes growing gentle and warm.

Lily experienced the effects of being near Jake almost immediately. The realization that she was so close to him that all she had to do was reach out and touch him caused her to tremble a little. She sat as far away as she dared without being obvious. Yet she was drawn to him like a homing pigeon to its place of rest.

"What did you pack?" Conversation was sure to help. And he had to do something to disguise his feelings.

"Pastrami sandwiches and homemade lemon meringue pie." She removed the cellophane and handed him a thick sandwich.

"Mustard?" He cocked one dark brow with the question.

"Your wish is my command."

"Your memory impresses me."

I'm glad something does, she mumbled to herself, feeling unexpectedly depressed. She didn't dare get close to Jake, even in the most innocent way. She yearned to curl up in his arms and nestle her head against the muscular cushion of his chest. Lily felt bone weary, having slept only a few hours the previous night. She looked away, fearing he would take one look at her and know what she was thinking.

"Aren't you going to eat something?" Jake asked. "I thought you said you were hungry."

"I am," she answered, somewhat defensively. Reaching inside the basket, she withdrew another thick sandwich, unwrapped it and took a bite. "There's a cold beer if you want one," she told him.

"Sure." Jake was surprised she'd think to bring one.

Lily brought one out for him and another for herself.

"I didn't know you liked beer. I thought you preferred wine."

"I do sometimes. Beer's good too. It's an acquired taste. Gram says it's good for what ails you."

Jake downed a large swallow and wiped his mouth off with the back of his hand. "Gram's right."

Lily took a much more delicate swig. The liquid felt cold all the way to her stomach. She took another bite of the sandwich. "My dad used to drink beer."

"You've never spoken much of your father."

"He died when I was young." Lily looked at the sails as they billowed in wind, avoiding eye contact with Jake.

"What about your mother?"

"I don't remember her," she said, her voice growing soft. "The pictures Gram gave me of her make me wish I had. She was really beautiful. But she died of complications following surgery. She had her appendix out, but apparently it had already burst."

"You must have been very young."

"Three. Gram took me in then because Dad traveled so much. I don't think Dad ever recovered from losing my mother. Gram says they loved each other like no two people she'd ever known, except her and Paddy. Yet my parents were nothing alike. Mom was delicate. From her pictures, she looks like a fragile princess. And Dad was this big hulk of guy—a lumberjack sort of fellow. I have wonderful memories of him. Whenever he'd come home it was like Christmas; he brought Gram and me the most marvelous gifts. I've saved every one. Mom and Dad's picture sits on my dresser. I'll show it to you sometime if you'd like."

The warm smile in Jake's eyes widened and spread to include his mouth. "You must resemble her." Lily was delicate, but not tiny the way she'd described her mother. Lily possessed a deep inner strength that he'd rarely seen in anyone else.

"Me?" Lily laughed. "No, I'm too much like my Dad. I've got this big nose and fat cheeks and ears that tend to stick out."

"You're lovely."

"Why, Jake, what a nice thing to say." She laughed and took another swallow of the beer. "When was the last time you had your eyes examined?" It felt good to laugh and tease him again. "What about your parents?"

"There's not much to tell. They're both still alive. I don't see them often. Unfortunately they tend to think of me as the black sheep of the family. My two brothers are successful. One's a bank executive and the other's a physician."

"And you're the almost famous writer." Lily was obliged to defend him. This past month when Lily had been seeing Rick and Rex had taught her how unfair it was to prejudge others by the balance of their checkbooks.

"No, I'm a cab driver and a failure. After all, they paid for four years of higher education for me that have completely gone to waste."

"It hasn't been wasted."

"In their eyes it has."

"You're a strong and solid man and if your parents don't see that, then I pity them." The intensity of her feelings surprised Lily. Jake was earthy and intelligent. A man of character and grit. He may have chosen a different path than his brothers, but that didn't make him any less a success.

"My mother would like you." His voice was softly gruff. "She'd see you as just the type who could reform me."

"But you don't want to be saved. Remember?" With a hint of resentment she tossed back his own words.

"You're right about that." But if anyone could ever do it, it would be Lily. A house, family and responsibilities wouldn't be half so bad if he shared his life with her. The change wouldn't come easy, but he would be more prone to consider it with her.

They finished their beer and sandwiches and Jake ate a thick slice of pie, praising her efforts.

The sun shone brightly against the horizon and the boat plowed smoothly ahead through the choppy waters. Gradually, Lily's head began to droop. The beer had added to her sleepiness, and now she fought to keep her eyes open but was slowly losing the battle. Her eyelids drooped as if someone had weighted them, and the sun bathed her in its golden warmth.

Intent on his duties, Jake didn't seem to notice until Lily started to slouch against his side. Instinctively he reached for her, looping an arm around her shoulders and pressing her weight to his side. The tenderness that gripped him was a shock. The sheer pleasure of holding her in his arms stabbed sweetly through him. He couldn't hold her and have it be any more natural. Pressing his face into the dark cloud of hair, he breathed in the fresh scent of her. She reminded him of summer wine.

Closing his eyes, Jake took in another deep breath and held it. He'd never told another living soul about his parents' disappointment in him. His love for Lily throbbed within him at the way she'd wanted to defend him. Her eyes had sparked with the fiery light of indignation. He recognized it since he'd provoked the same fire within her on more than one previous occasion.

A slow, lazy smile spread over his features. The wind changed directions and he expertly manipulated the canvas sails around to catch the power of the moving air.

Relaxed now, he stretched out his legs and crossed them at the ankles. A man could get accustomed to this. The woman he loved was in his arms and the sea was at his command.

Lily stirred, feeling secure and warm. Slowly she opened her eyes and realized the cause of this incredible relaxed sensation. Suspecting that any sudden movement would destroy the moment, Lily gradually raised her face to Jake. His serious eyes met hers.

The sails flapped in the breeze and still Jake didn't move. Lily remained motionless and the moment stretched out until she lost all concept of time. It could have been seconds or even minutes, she didn't know. Jake's beloved face was so close to hers that she could see clearly every line etched in his face by the kiss of the sun. While she was still trapped in the wonder of being in his arms, Jake smiled. Then, a fraction of an inch at a time, his mouth edged toward hers.

Their breath merged and Lily closed her eyes, surrendering to the incredible sensation. Ever so gradually, the firm texture of his mouth, exploring and mobile, eased onto hers. Lily felt her heart melt, but resisted the urge to lock her arms around his strong neck. Greedily she yearned for more but was unwilling to invite it. Only the day before, Jake had ardently claimed he hadn't wanted this. Yet here he was, holding her, kissing her and looking as though it would take all the forces of heaven and hell to drive them apart.

Their lips clung for what seemed a lifetime. When he dragged his mouth from hers, Lily didn't protest. Her response had to be carefully controlled. It would be tragic to destroy this moment. She kept her eyes closed and savored the feel of his breath as it continued to fan her lips. She gloried in its irregular rhythm, knowing that Jake was as affected by the kiss as she.

"Oh, Lily." Her name came on the tail end of a husky murmur. Jake bent his index finger and gently pressed it to her lips. "Did you sleep well?"

Her response was a faint nod.

"Good."

Unhurriedly, as if moving in slow motion, Jake lifted his arm from her shoulders. Lily shifted her weight and stretched. Sitting up straight, she smoothed her hands over her jean-clad thighs, all the while searching for something to say that would ease the electric tension.

"That shouldn't have happened."

Lily cast her gaze to the deck. "No, I suppose not."

"We should think about heading in. It's been a full afternoon."

Lily felt hurt and cheated. Why did Jake find it so objectionable to kiss her? Every time he did, it was wonderful. His touch stirred her blood and she experienced a tingling pleasure she was only beginning to understand.

"Okay," she mumbled. "If that's what you want."

"Don't you?"

"No. Yes. I don't know anymore. What's wrong with kissing me?" she asked him bluntly.

"Plenty. I'm not right for you." His brow narrowed into a heavy frown. "I'd never make you happy."

"I don't understand you," she cried, and to her disgrace, her voice broke. "How can anything that feels this good be wrong? I like it when you kiss me. I feel good inside. Tell me, Jake, why is that so wrong?"

"Because it is." His mouth had hardened and he stared straight ahead, effectively closing her out. Lily had seen that look often enough to realize that she might as well argue with a brick wall, for all the good it would do her.

With all the emotion of a mannequin, she reached for her jacket. A sudden chill went all the way to her bones. Jake was freezing her out as he'd done a hundred times over the past several weeks; but somehow it hurt more this time.

As they neared the marina, Jake momentarily gave her the helm and moved forward to lower the sails. The lump in the back of her throat had grown so large with the effort not to cry that she could barely swallow. Even breathing was difficult. Today was to have been their day. And now it was ruined, just as their every outing together had failed lately.

As they neared the dock, Jake noted a tear creep down the side of Lily's face. He started at the wet trail, stunned. She was crying.

"Lily, listen. I'm sorry. I shouldn't have kissed you."

"Stop it, Jake." Furious, she wiped the moisture from her cheek. "Why can't you be honest, for once? You wanted to kiss me. You've wanted it as much as I have for weeks. I don't know what you're trying to prove. I couldn't even begin to guess."

The *Lucky Lady* glided smoothly into her berth. Lily waited just long enough for the boat to steady before leaping onto the dock.

"Lily, wait." Jake jumped after her, pausing to secure the vessel. "I think we should talk." Hell, he didn't know what he could say, but seeing Lily cry was more than he could bear. He had to find some way to comfort her.

She turned to face him squarely. "No. Not today. I've got a date with Rick."

The words hit Jake with all the force of a freight train. So she was meeting his rich friend. Jake held her gaze and a muscle flexed convulsively in his lean jaw. Apparently it didn't bother her to go from one man's arms to another's. "Then what's keeping you around here?"

"You certainly wouldn't be interested in keeping me, would you?" Maybe it was cruel of her but she wanted him to experience just a little of the confusion and pain that was hers. "Rick, at least, likes me. He isn't hot and cold."

"Money can make up for a lot." Jake's stance was filled with rigid tension.

"In your case it . . ." She let the rest fade, regretting every word. Flinging angry barbs at each other would prove nothing.

"Say it," he shouted.

Sadly she shook her head. "Goodbye, Jake." With a determined effort, she turned and walked up the narrow dock. Every step took her farther from Jake and somehow Lily felt she'd never be coming back.

Jake watched her go, his fist knotted at his side. Half of him demanded that he race after her and turn her into his arms. The other half commanded that he stay exactly where he was. Against every dictate of his will and good sense, he'd done it again. He'd kissed her and regretted it, punishing Lily for his own weakness. It wasn't Lily's fault he found her utterly captivating. Nor was it her problem that he had happened to fall in love with her. But something had to be done. And quickly.

In the past, he'd toyed with the idea of packing up and moving down the coast. They couldn't go on this way. They were confusing one another, fighting their feelings, denying what they yearned for most. He had to get out of her life completely. There was no help for it. He had to leave.

Jumping back on the deck of his boat, Jake moved with determined strides. Now that he'd made up his mind, he felt better.

Below decks, he reached for the sea maps, charting his course down the California coast. He was a free man, no ties, no bonds. He could go without a backward glance. Except . . .

Jake paused. *Except.*

He slumped against the counter. He couldn't leave Lily. It would be like leaving a part of himself behind. Who the hell was he trying to fool? He loved her. Loved her enough to give up the precious freedom he'd struggled to maintain all these years.

He'd sell the boat before he'd lose Lily. The thought nearly paralyzed him. He'd meant it. Lily was worth ten thousand *Lucky Lady*'s.

When a man felt that deep an emotion for a woman there was only one option: marriage. He waited for the natural aversion to overtake him. It didn't. The startling fact was that it had a nice, homey sound to it.

His mind conjured up a house with a white picket fence around it. He could see Lily in the front yard planting flowers, pregnant.

That, too, had a nice feel to it. Jake hadn't thought of it much, but he'd like to have a son. And a daughter would be a joy if she looked anything like Lily.

Marriage, a family, responsibilities, credit cards, a regular job—those were all the things he'd despised over the years. Jake had claimed they weren't for him. But they would be if he had Lily at his side. All this time he'd had the gut feeling that Rex and Rick were wrong for her. Of course they were. *He* was the one meant for Lily. She loved him. Maybe she hadn't admitted it yet, but she would. In time, Jake could give her the fancy things she wanted. He'd even look forward to doing it.

Shuffling through his closet, Jake took out his best clothes. He'd shower and shave first so he'd look halfway decent. A man didn't ask a woman to be his wife every day of the week.

"Hi, Gram." Lily walked in the front door and pasted a plastic smile on her mouth.

Rocking in her chair, watching television, Gram glanced away from the screen. "You've been crying."

"It…just looks that way. I've got something in my eye."

"Like tears," Gram scoffed, slowly getting to her feet. "What happened?"

"Nothing." Lily's chin started to quiver and she could feel her control break. "Jake…kissed…me," she said, her voice quavering.

"Why, that's no reason to cry, child." Gram gave her a perplexed look as if she couldn't comprehend why Lily would find Jake's kiss so repulsive.

"I—I...know...but...he...doesn't...want...to."

"He'd hardly be kissing you if it wasn't what he wanted."

"You don't understand." Pride demanded that she wipe the tears from her face. "I'm so in love with him, Gram. But you know Jake. He doesn't want a woman in his life. Loving him has ruined everything. We've lost him."

Gram's look was thoughtful as she slipped her arm around Lily's waist and hugged her close. "Now dry those tears. You and me have weathered worse over the years. And as for losing Jake, we can't lose something we never had. Let Jake sort this out for himself. He's a smart man."

"I don't ever want to see him again."

A smile lifted the soft corners of the older woman's mouth. "You don't mean that. But I know how you feel. Paddy and me had some pretty good fights in our time."

"We didn't fight," Lily insisted. In some ways she wished they had. An argument would have cleared the air. It might even have brought out the truth and helped them find a solution—if there was one.

Slowly Gram walked into the kitchen and put on the kettle. "I'll make you a cup of Marmite."

"Thanks, Gram," she said solemnly, meaning for so much more than the offer of the hot drink. Gram was wise and good. Lily didn't know how she could seek her fortune through a wealthy man as if she'd been blind to the treasures that had been hers all her life.

The last thing Lily felt like doing was getting ready for her date with Rick. She wouldn't go out with him again. He was an okay fellow, but they had so little in common. Rick was recovering from a nasty divorce and needed someone to salve his ego. In a way they'd used each other, but that couldn't continue.

The doorbell chimed just when Lily was putting the finishing touches on her makeup. The telltale redness around her eyes had faded and she looked reasonably attractive.

Gram was watching television and Lily stuck her head around the corner to be sure that Gram had answered the door. With the television blaring, Gram often didn't hear the front door. It had gotten so bad that Jake had become accustomed to knocking once and letting himself in. At the thought of Jake, Lily drew in a ragged sigh. A tiny shudder went all the way through her body.

Rick stood awkwardly in the living room and Lily offered him her brightest smile. She wasn't looking forward to this evening. "I'll be with you in a minute."

"Take your time," he said, smiling back at her.

Lily dabbed French perfume behind her ear and took a deep breath. Tonight wouldn't be easy, but she wasn't going to be maudlin.

Gathering her purse and a light wrap, she joined Gram and Rick in the living room, forcing herself to smile.

Knowing Lily would be out with Rick, Jake waited for what he considered a reasonable amount of time before heading over to Gram's. Content now that he'd made his decision, he climbed inside his faithful taxi and absently ran his hand along the empty seat. He'd sell this car. That would have to be the first thing to go. While waiting, he'd scanned the newspaper. Finding a decent job shouldn't be too difficult. Engineers seemed to be in demand, and although his degree had several years' dust on it, he'd been a good student. An employer would recognize that soon enough.

On impulse, Jake stopped at a flower shop and picked up a small bouquet of flowers. He didn't know what kind they were; flowers were Lily and Gram's department. All he knew was that they seemed to impress a woman.

Humming, he eased to a stop in front of Gram's house, climbed out of the car and slapped his hand across the hood as he ventured past. He felt good. Once everything was straightened out with Lily, he'd be on cloud nine.

Gram answered his knock and he proudly shoved the flowers in her direction. "Is Lily home yet?"

"Are these for me or her?"

"Both."

"I'd say you're a bit late."

It wasn't like Gram to snap or grumble. Jake glanced at his watch. "It's barely ten."

"That's not the late I'm talking about."

"Is Lily home or not?" His own patience was running short.

"Not. I don't know what's come over you, but Lily came home in tears."

Shifting his weight from one foot to the other, Jake cleared his throat. He hadn't expected the third degree from Gram. "I came to apologize for that."

"And I'm telling you, you're too late."

A sudden chill went all the way through Jake. "What do you mean?"

"Rick was here earlier."

"I know." He hadn't liked it, either. All evening he'd battled down the image of Rick kissing Lily. He'd considered intercepting Rick, but he'd done that once to Lily and had promised himself he wouldn't again. No, she could have this one last dinner with Rick, but then it would be over.

"Only this time Rick didn't come alone."

Confused, Jake shook his head, not understanding Lily's grandmother. "How do you mean?"

"Rick came a-courting with a two-karat diamond ring in his pocket," Gram explained. "He's requested my permission to ask for Lily's hand."

Chapter Ten

I see," Jake said slowly. The words went sour on his tongue. He did indeed understand. Lily had finally achieved her goal. She'd found herself a wealthy man. Swallowing back the angry denial that trembled at the end of his tongue, Jake buried his hands deep inside his pants pockets. "I imagine Lily was happy?" He raised expectant eyes to Gram. The happy, carefree feeling that had been with him from the moment he'd decided to ask Lily to marry him slowly shriveled up and died.

"I can't rightly say. Rick planned on asking her at dinner this evening."

"Lily will accept." She'd be a fool not to, Jake knew.

"It's the best offer she's likely to get," Gram asserted, eyeing Jake in his best clothes. "But I'll tell her you were by."

"Don't." The lone word burst forcefully from his lips. "It wasn't anything important." He took a step backward and bumped into the front door. Abruptly he turned around and gripped the doorknob, his hold so punishing he wondered if he'd damage the knob. "No, on second thought you can mention that I was by. Tell Lily that I wish her and Rick every happiness."

"Do you want me to tell her anything else?" Gram encouraged with her usual astuteness. "You didn't bring these flowers for an old woman."

Jake's gaze fell on the elephant tusks mounted on the wall and the zebra-skin rug spread in front of the fireplace. Herbie, the shrunken head who Gram claimed was their spiritual protector, sat on the end table in its place of honor. Jake would miss all this and Gram with her African chants and wise old eyes. "No," he murmured sadly. There was nothing left to say. Lily's dreams had come true, and his worst nightmares were of his own making.

The following morning Lily sat down at the kitchen table with a mug of hot coffee. More than any time in recent history, she needed the caffeine. The evening with Rick had been a disaster from the very start. After he'd learned that she'd gone out with Rex, Rick had panicked and come to her with a ring and a marriage proposal. She didn't want to hurt him, but she couldn't marry him either.

The morning paper was spread across the tabletop and Lily mindlessly read the headlines. The colorful bouquet of flowers was in the vase where Gram usually kept her bills, but Lily didn't think much of it.

Gram had a habit of tossing things out when she got tired of looking at them.

"Where'd the flowers come from?" she asked, munching on a piece of toast.

Gram glanced up from the comic-strip section of the newspaper and grinned. "A secret admirer."

"Oh?" Gram had attracted more than one man. But to the best of her knowledge, Lily had never known her grandmother to see or talk of anyone except her beloved Paddy.

"Only my secret admirer couldn't decide if the gift was meant for me or you. He finally decided on me."

"And who could this indecisive fellow be? Thom the butcher? Or that new man who's been eyeing you at bingo?"

"Nope. It was Jake."

"Jake!" Lily did her utmost to disguise the wild happiness that shot through her. "Jake was here? When?"

Idly, Gram folded the newspaper to the crossword section and scrunched up her brow as she studied the fine print. "Late last night. It must have been close to ten."

Nearly too overwhelmed to speak, Lily stumbled over her words. "Why didn't you... What did he... Flowers?" She clenched the soft bathrobe at her throat. Jake here. Why, oh why, hadn't Gram said anything sooner?

"I don't know what he wanted. He didn't rightly say."

Standing, Lily pushed out the chair with the backs of her knees. "I'm going to get dressed. Did he stay long?"

"Five minutes or so. Not long." Gram didn't look up as her pencil worked furiously across the newspaper, filling in the words. "Just remember what I told you the first time we met Jake: you and he were meant for each other."

Lily found Gram's attitude totally bewildering. Years ago she'd given up trying to understand Gram's habits, but her grandmother's behavior was almost always rational. And rarely had Gram been more closemouthed. "Since Jake came by here, it would only be the polite thing to do to return the visit. Right?" She didn't wait for Gram to answer her. "He obviously had something on his mind or he wouldn't have come. I mean, it isn't like Jake to stop by unexpectedly." He did exactly that three or four times a week and Lily was grateful her grandmother didn't point it out.

Hardly caring what she wore, Lily dug through her drawer and found a pair of pink linen pants and a flowered top. A quick run of the brush through her hair left it looking shimmering and healthy.

At the marina the first thing Lily noticed was Jake's taxi with a For Sale sign propped against the dashboard. Lily stared at it with openmouthed disbelief. The money from the short story sale to the *New Yorker* had been good, but not enough to live on. Jake would never sell his source of income.

Hurrying now, she half-ran down the wooden dock that led to his slip. She spotted him almost at once, working on the deck, coiling a large section of rope around his arm. Her pace slowed. Now that she was here, there didn't seem to be anything to say. Although he was facing her, he didn't acknowledge her approach or give any indication that he'd seen her.

"Morning, Jake." She stood with her hands clenched together in front of her.

He ignored her, continuing to wind the thick rope around his arm, using his elbow as a guide.

"There's a For Sale sign on the cab."

"I know." He responded with iron-jawed grimness.

"But why?"

"It's for sale." His voice held no welcome.

Lily could see that this conversation wasn't going to get them anywhere if she continued to question him. "Gram said you were by the house last night."

"I was."

If he didn't stop with that stupid rope and look at her soon, she was going to rip it out of his arms. "The flowers are lovely."

Jake's mouth tightened. "Consider them a good-bye present."

Her heart pounded wildly in her ears. "Good-bye?"

"Yeah, I'm moving down the coast."

"This is all rather sudden, isn't it?"

"I've been thinking about it for some time."

Lily's hands rose challengingly to her hips. "You'd move just to spite me, wouldn't you?"

For the first time, he halted and glanced up at her, his eyes a brilliant green. His feet were braced slightly apart as if anticipating a fight. "You're not making any sense. I'm moving because..."

"Because you're afraid."

Jake snorted. Inwardly, he admitted that she was probably right. He couldn't be around Lily without wanting her and the best thing for them both was to remove the temptation. "I've fought in the jungles of

Vietnam, tangled with drunks who couldn't afford to pay their fare, and listened to your grandmother sing an African chant over my head. Believe me, you have little reason to accuse me of cowardice." That, too, was a half-truth. Just being close to Lily caused him to tremble. What had made perfect sense the day before seemed utter stupidity now. He loved her, yes. But that didn't make it right for them to consider marriage.

"You're going away because of me."

"Yes!" Jake shouted, feeling angry and unreasonable. "I have this particular quirk about being seen with a married woman."

"I'm not married."

"Not yet, but you will be. Gram told me about Rick's proposal."

She held up her bare left hand, fanning her fingers. "I turned him down."

"That wasn't a smart move."

"I don't love Rick."

"That's your problem, Lily. You've got too much conscience. Loving him isn't necessary. Rick can give you all the those fancy things you want."

"He can't give me what I want the very most."

"Give him time."

"Even that won't work," she assured him.

"And what is it that you want so badly?"

"You."

His dark eyes found hers, stunned and staring. "You don't mean that."

"I love you, Jake Carson."

"I don't have the money to buy you a fat diamond."

"A simple gold band will do." For every argument Jake presented, she would have an answer. She hadn't come this far to let him slip away.

"My home is right here. There isn't going to be any fancy house." *Except maybe one with a white picket fence and a row of flowers at the front.*

"In case you hadn't noticed, I love the *Lucky Lady*. We'll live right here."

"There won't be room when the children come." He tossed another argument at her.

"Then we'll buy a bigger boat."

"I told you before that I can't give you the things Rick will." He didn't know why he continued to argue. He loved her.

"No, you can't. But I've learned how meaningless diamonds can be. I love you, Jake, and if you love me back, I'd consider myself the wealthiest ex-piano player in town."

Jake's defenses relaxed visibly, the rope fell unheeded to the deck and he held out a hand to Lily, guiding her safely aboard the *Lucky Lady*'s deck and into his arms. He buried his face in her hair and held her for several minutes, just breathing in the fresh fragrance of her. "I love you so damn much that part of me would have died to stand by and watch you marry Rick."

"Then why would you have let me?" Even now she couldn't understand his reasoning.

"Because I discovered that in my own way I wanted to give you all those material things you deserved. But in order to do that I had to let you go."

Lovingly, Lily cupped his face. The strong, proud features seemed to intensify with each word.

A weary sigh came deep from within Lily. "The only thing I'll ever want is you."

"I am yours." A great weight seemed to leave his voice. "I have been since that night in the attic and probably long before then, only I refused to acknowledge it." His strong arms held her closer as if he feared she would escape him.

Lily's dark eyes gleamed with happiness. "Gram was right."

"About what?"

"Before I left this morning, she told me that you and I were destined to be together."

Unable to resist any longer, Jake tenderly kissed the corner of her mouth. "How could she be so sure of that?"

Lily's hands toyed with the hair at the back of his neck. "Do you remember the day we met in front of the Wheaton and how Gram chanted over you?"

His mouth found her cheek. "I'm not likely to forget it."

"Gram was sealing our fate. That was a fertility rite. We're doomed to live a long, happy life. And from what Gram said, we're going to need a very large boat in the years to come."

Jake chuckled. "I can live with that," he told her, just before his hungry mouth claimed hers.

COMING NEXT MONTH

FAMILY AFFAIR—Rita Rainville
Brady wanted to marry the right woman—Sara Clayton. And
with the help of five elderly friends and one orangutan, he set out
to win her love.

GIFT OF THE GODS—Judith McWilliams
Rescuing her teenage "charge" from the hands of wealthy Greek
Philip Stephanos turned out to be easier than rescuing herself—
especially when Sophie discovered she didn't want to be rescued!

A MAN FOR SYLVIA—Sue Santore
What was the mystery of the velvet painting? Could it be behind
the accidents befalling Sylvia? With Craig's help, Sylvia probed
the puzzling secrets of the picture—and her heart.

THE FOREVER KIND—Karen Young
When Jill's little boy disappeared, it was old friend
Sam Halloran to the rescue. But finding Josh was easier than
convincing Jill to take another chance on love—and Sam.

FOR EACH TOMORROW—Curtiss Ann Matlock
It had been years since Quent left town. Now he was back—a
dashing Oklahoma Ranger—and after Cassie's heart. Cassie
didn't want to give it to him. But she soon learned that in order to
gain, you had to risk—and that the reward was worth the price.

NO QUESTIONS ASKED—Lynnette Morland
Conn Tomelty, celebrated journalist, was doing a story on
Lifeline, a disaster relief organization. But what he really wanted
to research was its newly appointed director, Rosalie Madden.

AVAILABLE THIS MONTH

UNLIKELY LOVER
Diana Palmer

THE CASTAWAYS
Frances Lloyd

FRIENDS—AND THEN SOME
Debbie Macomber

HEAVENLY MATCH
Sharon De Vita

THE EYES OF A STRANGER
Terri McGraw

HERO ON HOLD
Glenda Sands

$\mathcal{D}$ Silhouette Desire

**Available
January 1987**

NEVADA
SILVER

The third book in the exciting
Desire Trilogy by Joan Hohl.

The Sharp brothers are back, along with
sister Kit...and Logan McKittrick.

Kit's loved Logan all her life and, with a little
help from the silver glow of a Nevada night,
she must convince the stubborn rancher that
she's a woman who needs a man's love—not
the protection of another brother.

Don't miss *Nevada Silver*—Kit and
Logan's story and the conclusion
of Joan Hohl's acclaimed
Desire Trilogy.

DT-C-1